SUNDROP DAGGER

BLADES OF VENGEANCE

ROWAN THALIA
JENÉE ROBINSON

Rebekah,
I ♡ your
face!
— ♡ Jenée Robinson

Zelle

Wind whips through the long hall between my cellblock and the stone wall. With a grimace, I pull on the warmest cape I have. Though it's thread-bare, it still serves a purpose. Carefully, I straighten the cover on my cot and slide on a pair of slippers. Crossing the small space, I pick up my chalk and mark another day.

Then it dawns on me, "Happy birthday to me," I sigh as I sketch a tiny cake next to the calendar with the chalk. Relishing the moment of peace, I try my best not to let my jailers know I'm awake.

Moments of happiness have been few and far between since mother traded me to the Fae to settle her debts a few years ago. Who would have thought I'd long for the cloistered life she provided someday? Was she the best mother in the land? No, but she was all I had.

Sadly, today also marks another year in this Fae prison.

"Zelle," my mother's voice floats down the cell block, "Time to get up, deary."

1

Resigned to sit through another visit with a fake smile, I straighten my dress and smooth my long, blonde braid. With a quick swipe of my hand, the drawing disappears. If I seem unsightly, my mother's visit will go poorly. I don't relish her coming, but I enjoy that someone still chooses to spend time with me.

The rusty hinges squeak as the door opens, and bright light floods the room, blinding me.

"There's my girl," Mother says in a high-pitch squeal, pulling me in for a hug. "Happy birthday, Zelle. I've received good news from the King—he has a surprise for you today!"

"Will I be able to come home?" I ask, looking into her eyes.

"No, darling. I'm sorry," she replies in a sad tone. "But there is a tall tower on the edge of the castle over-looking the barrier between our world and this one. The King has agreed that you've proved loyal and may move there. Furthermore, he's granted you leave from your duties today to settle in."

"What's so special about moving me to another tower, Mother?" I ask, returning my eyes to the floor to avoid seeing her reaction to the slight dig. Seems I'll be living in the sky once more. I search the stones for why my fate always looks so dim.

"Well, I haven't been there, but I was told there is a proper bed." Mother lifts my chin.

"A real bed?" I cut in excitedly. I haven't had a good night's sleep since coming here. My cot is hard on one end and lumpy on the other.

"Hush, Zelle, you know it's rude to interrupt while others are speaking. But yes, there's a real bed and a kitchen."

The kitchen is even better news than the bed. One of the things I longed for the most was homemade bread. They feed us regularly down here in the dark cells, but the mash is barely edible.

"Will you come with me?" I question.

"Sadly, no. You know I can't leave the mortal world. I'll still visit from time to time, maybe even more often, since I won't have to come to this dirty place to see you," Mother purses her lips. "Anyway, I thought you'd be happy to hear the news from me. Happy Birthday, Zelle," she says with a smile that doesn't reach her eyes.

"Thank you, Mother," I choke as she squeezes me a little too hard.

"One little song for Mother?" she asks.

I sigh before starting my healing song. I knew she was going to ask. It only takes one hint of a wrinkle on her face for her to have me erase the mark as if it was never there. The older I get, the more I wonder if my worth lies only in this power. Once my song is finished, she removes her arms from around me and crosses the room in a rush.

"Zelle is ready for her move to the tower," she calls the guards.

There's an echo of keys jangling before footsteps are near. "Be a good girl and enjoy your time off. The King has granted the day and night there before you are to return back to your duties. You may even get a glimpse of those floating lights that always appear on your birthday."

"Yes, Mother," I nod. Before I can say another word, she is gone, and the guards are sneering at me.

"Why the King would allow scum like you in his tower is beyond me, but here," he says, thrusting a rag toward me. "Tie this around your eyes. You aren't to see the way to the tower."

I do as he commands, the foul cloth's stench fills my nose, and I have to swallow the bile that threatens to spill from my lips.

"Do I have to touch her?" Wren grouches.

"Yes, I handed her the rag, so you have to guide her. A deal is a deal," Altair says in a gruff tone.

"Fine," Wren huffs, and a hand wraps around my bicep before he all but drags me from my cell. I stumble and almost fall a few times. Wren's voice is gloating as he calls me an idiot for the tenth time. Doesn't he understand that I can't see when there is something in the path? He is really a moron.

I didn't ask for any of this. I was content to stay in my cell or work like a typical day. This special treatment definitely has a catch. I don't know what the catch is yet. To make matters worse, I have no doubt that I will have to bandage up my feet once they deposit me into the tower. Of course, I'm curious about how to get up there, but I don't dare ask.

"OK, Altair, you go up first. Once you send the bucket back, I'll put her in," Wren says.

The only sounds are the wheel's squeak and the

guard's grunting. The wheel screeches louder until it stops. Suddenly a hand pushes me forward, and I fall face-first to the grassy ground.

"Grab the fucking bucket, then turn around and sit. I will hoist you up. Once you're at the top, Altair will help you into your new home. There is no other way in or out of the tower," Wren grits out through his teeth.

"What have I done to you to be treated so poorly?" I question but obey.

He answers with his hand across my face. "I didn't give you permission to speak to me."

Covering the sore spot with my palm, I bite my tongue. My cheek stings, but I know that I got off easy. Not one Fae in the Kingdom of Wolgast has any love for me. Mother has always been good at pretending, but I see the glances she throws when she doesn't think I'm looking.

"Find the rope and hold on. If you fall out, the King will have my head. For some reason, he likes you."

I want to scream and rebel at his words, but it won't do me any good. He's wrong. The King doesn't like me. He uses me just as my mother does for my magic hair. What better way to keep your slave working than to give them a small luxury? On days like this, I long to be normal.

After an awkward moment, I'm able to get my ass in the bucket. Although I don't understand why I have to be blindfolded, won't I be able to see the kingdom from the tower? The Fae rarely seem to think these punishments through. It's all just a mind game. The bucket

5

jerks and swings, slamming me into the brick wall as I rise. Leaning my head up, I'm able to see just enough to push off with my feet when needed and avoid any head bonks.

The bucket stops, and I let out the breath I was holding. Part of me thought they might drop me on purpose. Altair's hand grips mine as he drags me over the ledge and into my new home. I'm left standing as Altair hoists up Wren. The two have been assigned as my guards for the last year. Neither one fancies me, but Altair is a little nicer.

"Close the shutters," Wren demands as he pushes me forward.

I take a small step, using my other senses to get a feel of what's in store. The room smells like fresh linen and sunshine. Breathing the scent in, I almost cry. It's already a massive change from the mildewy dungeons. My blindfold is removed, and I blink twice.

"Your quarters." Altair swings his arm in an arc. "The only window you'll be allowed to look out is that one," he points out. "It faces the border between lands and the main entrance to the kingdom. Wren and I will stay in the smaller room through that red door. The rest of this floor is yours. Do not under any circumstances open the shutters to any other window—is that clear?"

"Yes." I bob my head. I've learned the hard way it's best to stay in line with these two.

"Good, we're going to clean up. Look around your space. You've got the afternoon off," Altair says as he and Wren walk toward the red door. I'm sure the window at the top is for them to watch me.

I stand still until their door swings shut. Once the guards are out of sight, I giggle and spin in a circle. Being in a room that doesn't touch my fingers when I spread my arms sends me over the moon. Dizzy from turning, I flit around the perimeter of the main room. This room has a small kitchen and a sitting area next to the window. A connecting room holds a large bed on one side and as close to a bathroom as I could get on the other, separated by a privacy screen. Overjoyed by the thought of running water, I rush over.

There's a spelled fountain, which fills a stone sink that cascades into the oversized tub. Hidden behind the tub is what the Fae designed as a toilet. I have yet to have the faintest idea how the contraption works, but I do know whatever you deposit in it disappears when you close the lid.

I scout the space for clean clothing because I don't want to dirty my new bed. In the trunk, I find a couple of serviceable frocks. Wasting no time, I close the privacy screen and undress. When I step into the bath, I almost faint. Warm, clean water is like a gift from above. Sinking down, I hold my breath and lay under the surface for as long as my lungs allow. When I finally pop back up, I lean against the edge. Baths are a treat, but I've just realized I'll need to wash the long locks that created this whole mess for me in the first place.

Uncoiling my hair from its braid, I sigh. "I wonder if

the King will still allow Gwynfor to help me tame these unruly tresses?"

My voice goes unanswered, of course, and I set to washing. An hour later, my arms and back are tired, so I step out and change into the new-to-me dress. I'd like to check out the kitchen, but I need a nap after washing. Falling upon my bed, I pull the blankets up and close my eyes.

W hen I wake, the light has moved across the room, leaving me in the shadows. It must be late afternoon. Stretching, I sit up and survey the space. This side of my new home is shuttered, so no light seeps in. Hopefully, I still have a view from the kitchen. Draping my unbound hair over one arm, I quickly cross the cool, stone floor.

"Thank the stars," I whisper as I approach the window.

As Mother stated, the view is of the border between the Faerie and Mortal worlds. The line isn't visible from the other side but presents as a purple haze from here. Sitting on the small, padded bench below the window, I prop my hands on my fists. Now I see why I'm not allowed to open any other shutters. From this vantage, I can only glimpse the kingdom's guard shack, main gate, and front walls. Everything else is behind my tower.

"Maybe I'll make myself a cake," I say out loud to fill the emptiness.

Just as I turn, I hear a commotion from below.

Curious, I lean out, trying to get a clear view of the gates as they open slowly. A group of around twenty guards enters. In the middle of their circle, they pull a barred cart. Poking out of the sides are the largest pair of white-feathered wings I've ever seen. Placing one hand on my mouth, I gasp, "Have they captured an angel?"

Heart breaking for the new prisoner, I try my best to get a clear image of the face. My efforts are paid in full when he braces his hands on the bars and looks up. He's the most beautiful male I've ever seen, with cropped, brown hair and piercing, green eyes. His gaze bores into me and makes it seem like he knows I want to see him. The moment is fleeting as a guard notices and slams his baton on the angel's hands. A lump forms in my throat when I notice the blood and bruises covering his form. King Thayer is known for collecting all magical creatures to serve in his court as slaves—but what use does he have for a godly one?

I could heal him if I wasn't stuck in this tower. That would ease my heartache just a little. Somehow my gift is now a new form of torture. I sink down from the window as the tears start to flow. What good is this healing gift if I can't use it for those who deserve it?

After a few moments, I wipe my face clean and return to baking a cake. Hopefully, the tiny kitchen would hold everything I'd need. A smile touches my lips, and I let out a happy squeal when I open the cupboards and see all the baking supplies. I know this is another form of manipulation by the King, but I will enjoy it all the same. It will also distract me from thoughts about the broken angel.

Moving an upturned bowl, a small shriek escapes my lips when a little, green blur races past me.

"Quiet down in there!" Wren yells from the guard room.

I don't reply. It would just give the cranky guard an excuse to backhand me again. I raise my hand to my chest as if the action will soothe my heart. Nothing is ever as it seems here. Not that my previous life was one of pleasure, but at least I wasn't a slave.

Determined to enjoy my birthday, I peek around for the little creature who zoomed past me but can't find it. It sure would be nice to have a pet for companionship. I'll have to keep an eye out for the little guy. Smiling at the thought, I set back to work on the cake.

Once I have the batter ready, I search for a pan. For once, my efforts aren't fruitless. I find the perfect pan for my cake and a mini pan that would be just right for my guest. There's no creature around that doesn't like cake, right?

With everything ready to bake, I light the fire for the stove. It doesn't take long to get up to temperature, another Fae magic, I'm sure. Getting more excited, I pop the cakes in the oven and wander back toward the desk to sketch to pass the time. I'm tempted to search for my guest, but I hope the cake's smell will lure it out.

The pencil in my hand feels natural, as if I never stopped before I was traded into this sad excuse of existence. I let my mind wander as the pencil floats over the paper and the image of a lantern comes to life.

Before long, there is a trail of them just like the ones I see on the night of my birthday each year.

Lost in memories of the lights, the smell of the cake brings me back to today. I still have frosting to make. A picture in my mind forms, and I decide on pink and purple frosting with yellow accents to brighten up my dull life. My hand mixes as my mind wanders. At the same time that the frosting is finished, the cakes are ready, so I pull them out to rest on the window sill, careful not to glance out of the window and catch more heartache.

My hair gets caught on the chair leg as I start toward the desk again. So, I decide it is time to brush it and re-braid it.

Mother cut a lock of my hair once, hoping to carry my gift with her on her travels. But the piece turned brown in her hand and on my head, rendering it useless. Since that time, cutting off my hair has been forbidden. My hair is more important than I am. With a sigh, I start putting it back up in its braid. I hum a little tune, barely audible, so my jailers don't have a reason to yell again.

Tasks seem unending. After finishing my hair, it's time to frost my cakes. I take my time, enjoying the fact that there's no reason to rush. This is the first birthday in years that I am free to do as I please, and I'm not taking it for granted.

The purple frosting smooths over the cake effortlessly. With a frosting bag I made, I pipe pink around the base and the top edge. The last color is yellow. Joy filling my heart, I leave it to my hand to decide the pattern, and it doesn't disappoint. I stand back and admire my handiwork. In the middle of the cake, there is a golden sun. I can almost feel the warmth radiating, even though it's only a cake. With a spring in my step, I start on the mini cake. Of course, it should match. Once I'm satisfied, I sit them on the little dining table, searching for something to cook for dinner.

All this work has left me hungry, and my stomach rumbles in agreement. As I dig through the cupboards, the door to the guard room is thrown open. Startled, I look over to see Wren stroll in with a sour face and a plate full of food. He grunts and throws it on the table, almost hitting my cake.

Barely glancing at me, he doesn't speak a word before he leaves as quickly as he came. Watching the door in astonishment, I grip the edge of the counter. Once the door is locked behind him, the words slip from my lips, "Thank you."

Wren may be an asshole, but it was as if he knew I required something to eat.

The savory scent wafting in the air drags me across the room. Everything on the plate looks appealing, but I can't decide where to start. I haven't seen food like this in so long that I have to restrain myself from diving in too fast and giving myself a tummy ache. Sitting down, I take a few bites, enjoying the sweet fruits and mild cheeses, when I notice the green blur again.

Hoping it will come closer. I don't move a muscle. Holding my breath, I wait to see if the food or cakes lure it out. My actions pay off, and a cute, little chameleon appears from under the table. It freezes when it notices me and changes colors to match the table's wood. I can make out his outline as his tongue shoots out and takes a piece of the mini cake.

I whisper, "I made that for you."

He takes another bite and reveals himself to me, his eyes rolling curiously.

"I'm Zelle. You can stay here with me if you'd like. It would be nice to have a friend; I've never had one," I say, placing a palm up on the table.

My new, little friend takes a few paces toward me cautiously.

"I won't hurt you," I promise, keeping my tone light.

He closes the distance, placing a little foot on my palm as if he understands my intent. A tiny spark of hope blooms within my chest as I slowly bring the chameleon closer. His foot grips my finger, but his body relaxes in my palm.

"Well, hi," I giggle. "How about I call you Pascal?"

His little eyes blink, and I smile. My stomach growls again, and I carefully set Pascal back on the table. "I've got to eat," I say. "Feel free to take anything you like."

Pascal looks up at me before he races over to the windowsill. Settling in, I grab the chicken leg from the plate and take a juicy bite as I watch my friend. Pascal lingers on the window frame watching the sky. All at once, his tongue darts out, and he catches an insect. He and I enjoy our meal this way until both bellies are full.

"I hope you enjoyed your dinner as much as I did," I lean back in my chair. My plate is empty, save the chicken bones, but the cake is untouched.

"I think I'll save the cake for later," I stand and cover the cake with a large glass bowl. "Shall we watch the sunset together? Tonight the sky will light up with lanterns!" I offer a finger, and Pascal climbs onto my hand.

The bench near the window has a cushion, so I cross my legs and get comfortable. Pascal perches on my shoulder, watching the sky turn blue to purple and black. The darkness doesn't last long before thousands of yellow lamps float from the horizon upward. They seem to dance and wave, calling me to join them.

Zelle

A loud noise startles me. I must have fallen asleep. Looking around the now-dark room, I listen for the origin of the bumping. The floorboards shake, and I drop to the ground. Pascal scampers to one of the shuttered windows and makes a strange click.

"What is it?" I tiptoe toward him.

Before I get to his side, the shutter opens. Slowly, I creep toward the forbidden opening. When I finally gain the courage to look out, nothing is there. This is my chance. I scoop up Pascal, wrap my hair around the flagpole, and spelunk down the side of the tower.

My feet hit the mossy ground. Before I can blink, I'm transported to my old cell block. A flutter of wings draws my attention, and I run toward the sound. The angel! Approaching the last cell, I feel his green eyes bore a hole into my heart. Determined to rescue him, I search the walls for a key.

"Zelle," he whispers.

When I wake, I can still hear the angel's voice. A shiver runs down my spine as the cold, morning air blows through the window. Frozen on the bench, I pat

16

my cheeks, trying to force myself back to reality. The dream felt so real. A tear escapes my eye as the image of the angel clouds my mind.

Heart aching, I rise and make my way into the bedroom. My feet feel leaden, each step taking more and more effort. Finally, I arrive at the bedside. With the last of my energy, I flop down and stare at the ceiling. Everything hurts from sleeping on the bench, but nothing so much as my soul. I must find a way to help him. "Girl, are you awake?"

Altair peeks into the room. "Your duties resume today. Get dressed and come to the kitchen."

With a groan, I sit back up and assess myself. The dress I wore yesterday is still clean, so I stand and smooth the apron. My back aching, I wrap my hair around my torso and sing.

"Flower, gleam, and glow
Let your powers shine
Make the clock reverse
Heal what has been hurt
Bring back what once was mine."

My hair glows, and my body tingles as the magic removes my aches. Not knowing what the day will bring, I slowly enter the kitchen. Wren stands near the closed shutters, and Altair holds a small, sweet bread in his outstretched hand.

"Eat. We need you strong for the day. Many need your gift," he sighs.

Nodding, I take the bread and eat quickly. Altair hands me a fairy drop of water, and I also pop that into my mouth. The bubble feels hard as a rock until it melts in my mouth and releases cool, refreshing water to slate my thirst.

Without warning, a blindfold is placed over my eyes again. The creak of the shutters opening is the only warning I get before I'm pushed into the bucket. The process is tiring, and I almost cry thinking about how this will become another routine I'll have to endure daily.

"We'll bring you back to your old cell daily for your healing duties. Once we enter the building, I'll take off the cloth," Altair states as he grasps my arm. Wren only grunts and grabs the other arm.

Both Fae lead me down the slope with more care than yesterday. I don't thank them because I don't want them to return to treating me poorly. The damp scent of the cellblock washes over us when they open the door, and I shiver. After stepping inside, my eyes are unbound as promised.

"You take her to the cell, and I'll start bringing in the hurt," Wren barks out.

As Altair takes me down the hall, each prisoner we pass whispers a hello. I've treated most of them numerous times. With a faint smile, I return their greetings. Most work down in the mines, but a select few are treated as palace slaves. That might seem like a better job, but it isn't. The King is cruel and twisted. Those who he interacts with never come away unscathed.

"Sit." Altair pushes me into my old cell, and I almost cry. I had hoped never to see these walls again.

Before I can dwell in self-pity, the clip-clop of hooves hitting the stone floor approaches. Biting my lip, I wipe my tears and see Kain limp into the cell. His silvery-white mane is matted with blood, and his back leg is drawn up. Rising, I run a hand over his nose in greeting. He chuffs a long breath into my hand and pushes his head against me, careful not to hurt me with his horn.

"I'm happy to see you," I whisper as I wrap my hair around his body. "Although I wish it weren't so frequent since it means you've been hurt."

Kain chuffs again, nodding his head up and down in agreement. The unicorn is part of the Queen's chariot team. He's a regular visitor since the Queen has a heavy hand with her whip. This time, his injuries exceeded beatings. With a tear in my eye, I sing, watching my hair glow as it turns his bloody body back to its natural white shine.

Tiptoeing to the cell door, I check to ensure the guards are nowhere near since I know Kain will want to shift. None of the Fae realize he's a shifter. It's our secret. Satisfied he won't be seen, I turn and offer the robe I keep in the corner for Kain. The bulk behind me lightens, and a hand takes the garb from me.

"You can turn around now," Kain's voice washes over me like cool rain.

"Let me look at your injuries now that you've shift-ed," I state as I face him.

A lock of his long, blond hair covers his eyes, but he sits and offers me his leg. I take it and move it to get a better look. The wince he gives in return tells me all I need to know. I usually have to heal him again in human form when he's been hurt badly.

"What happened?" I ask as I wind my hair about him."

"She made me fight a werewolf," he grits. "When I killed it with my horn, she beat me."

"Oh, Kain." I sit next to him as I hum my healing incantation.

"It's nothing. I'm sorry I missed your birthday. Happy birthday, Zelle. Where did they take you? You smell different, and that's a new dress, isn't it?" Kain wraps an arm around my shoulder and whispers in my ear so that we aren't found out.

"The King has sent me to the tower for my living quarters now," I answer quietly. "I don't know what to make of it, but I was able to bake myself a cake!"

"The tower facing the entrance?" Kain's eyes light up.

"Yes, why?"

"That's the furthest point from the Queen. You should be safe there," he answers before rising. "The guards are coming now. I can smell Wren."

"Please be more careful today," I turn, knowing he'll need privacy.

"Never, every hurt brings me here," Kain's voice holds a smile, and my heart thumps wildly.

Not a moment later, Wren darkens the doorway. He moves past me and takes Kain by the lead rope. Hooves click on the stones, fading as Kain is led from the room.

As soon as they're gone, an unfamiliar scent fills the

room, almost like freshly baked snickerdoodle cookies. My stomach rumbles, and I turn only to take a step back when a large feather brushes my face.

"The angel," I say without meaning for him to hear.

"A fallen one, but yes," the green eyes from my dream drop to my level. "I'm Xavier."

"Zelle," I squeak.

There's something about this angel that makes me weak in the knees. If I'm being honest; the unicorn has almost the same effect. I can ignore the feeling with Kain since I have to attend to his modesty so often. I don't know if I can do the same with Xavier.

"I don't see any medical supplies. How do you heal?" Xavier asks, arching a brow at me.

"You're an angel. Can't you heal yourself?" I snap back as I take a step toward him.

"Fallen," he repeats with a wince that makes me sorry for my bumbling mouth.

Cheeks flaming, I press forward. "Where are you hurt?"

I glance toward him quickly before returning my eyes to the ground since the last time his green eyes had shaken me to my core.

He laughs softly, "Maybe it's better to ask where I'm not hurt. Being wrangled out of the sky isn't graceful, and I wasn't given the warmest of welcomes when I arrived."

"That's par for the course," I say, daring eye contact.

"Zelle, hurry up. We have more for you to heal!" Altair yells from the hall, making me jump. After all this time, you'd think I would be used to their loud tones, but I'm not.

With a sigh, I move closer to Xavier. One of his wings is bent at an awkward angle. Without thinking, I begin to wrap my hair around the damaged appendage. With a gentle hand, I make sure the strands are secure. Wetting my lips, I open my mouth and stall when Xavier places his hand on mine.

"What kind of medicine is this?" he questions.

"The magic hair kind," I shrug and start to sing before I can say anything else stupid. My hair begins to glow, and Xavier's face lights up in wonder. After a few moments, the glow fades, and his wing returns to its proper form.

"What next? The guards will be here soon, best not to wait much longer to tell me," I whisper as I unwrap my hair.

"Just my hand. Everything else is just sore, but nothing I can't live with," Xavier comments as he holds his palm up.

I wrap it up with a slight nod, much like the wing. It doesn't take long for my song to be complete, and the hand heals. My gut wrenches at the quickness. There is an unspoken attraction sparking between us that's overwhelming.

"Next time, you'll have to explain this magic and how it came to be."

"Let's hope there isn't another time," I say with a sad smile. "I may have a simple job here, but it is not easy."

"How did you get here?" Xavier turns toward me, loosening a single feather that drifts between us.

Before I can answer, the guards reappear and pull the angel from my cell. I want to ask them how many more are waiting but think better of it. What if my questions upset them, and they decide not to take me back to the tower? The thought of staying here another night makes my stomach roll.

Every minute after seeing Xavier seems to drag on and on. It isn't lost on me that there's no shortage of hurt and battered today. I can't help but wonder what so many had done to have so much wrath brought down on them. When Wren and Altair popped in, I knew my day was done.

"Time to return to the tower. You know the drill, turn around," Wren orders, taking one step toward me.

Skin crawling at the thought of the smelly rag, I do as he says. Wren makes quick work of it, and my eyes are bound once more in moments. Forcefully, he turns me back to what I think is the opening of the cell. When my toe connects with metal, I suppress a scream and allow him to pull me along. These assholes must have decided that yesterday's path wasn't rough enough on my bare feet. What better way to torture the girl that can heal?

Refusing to show any emotion, I bite my lip all the way back to the tower. I know that any cry of pain is what they long for, and I refuse to give them the satisfaction. I'm released roughly, and the pulley squeak tells me we have reached the tower. Regardless of circumstance, I'm almost giddy, as the day of healing so many has worn me down.

After a loud thud, I'm pushed forward. Can't the King find another way to get us to the top?

"Foot up, get in the bucket," Wren commands.

Without hesitation, I do what he says. As I am raised back to my new but better living conditions, I hold on. Rough hands tug me into the window. Once I gain my footing, the rag is removed.

"Go bathe, the stink of death is filling the tower," Altair sneers, and I open my mouth in surprise. Usually, he's a little gentler, but it seems he's also had his fill of this day.

I give him a slight nod and head to the little room that has quickly become a sanctuary. The bathroom is the only place where I have any privacy from my jailers. The spring-fed waters are a boon, even being a slave. Everything in me aches. Yes, I healed those that needed it, but who will heal me?

By the time I had the tub full, both guards were in their little room asleep, their snores audible through the door. Rolling my eyes, I disrobe and step in. It's pure heaven. The hot liquid was just what I needed after this long day. Leaning back to relax, soaking my hair and body, I hum the healing incantation. The water glows with magic, and all of the pain resides.

Realizing what a chore it will be to dry and brush my hair after all the prisoners I've seen today, I grumble. My golden hair is now stained brown or red in places. Resigned to the task, I begin to lather up, grateful for the running water.

When I'm about halfway into the task, Pascal skids across the tile floor.

"Pascal," I giggle as he races forward and stops on the tub's edge. A smile spreads across my lips at my little friend. I could swear that he was smirking. "I'm glad to see you haven't deserted me. Once I'm clean, I'll get us some more cake."

His little, green head bobs up and down in acknowledgment. Communicating with a reptile would be absurd anywhere else, but I'm sure he's got a tinge of Fae magic. He skitters towards the little shelf and curls up with a yawn. Who knew that chameleons were so clever? He knows my hair will take time to clean and seems happy to stay near me as I work.

Rinsing takes less time than washing. My hair is soap-free in record time. On a whim, I decided to sling it out the tower window to air dry. It would be faster than trying to do it myself, and the cover of night should hide my hair from prying eyes. Stepping across the floor, I twist as much water as possible before gathering it up and throwing it out the open window.

Since my hair is hanging from the window, there is little to do. So I grab a cup of water and sit on the bench. The stars twinkle, and a cool breeze rustles the leaves of the nearby forest. Yearning for a wide-open space, I lean out of the window. At this angle, it's almost the same as being outside.

I can't remember a time in my life where I wasn't trapped in a small living space. Since being sold into slavery, I've often questioned my backstory. How could a mother sell their own child? Unless I was never hers. My heart thumps wildly. Come to think of it, I look nothing like Gothel. Could she have stolen me, as she stole the very Fae magic which earned her debt?

Pacing the room as much as my hair will allow, I sift through memories trying to uncover clues. So many things raise more questions. I have fragments of memories of a couple with crowns on their heads. Mother always told me I dreamed of being a princess so often that I'd convinced my mind to make the memories—but what if I didn't make them up?

"Zelle!" I jump, not expecting to hear my name.

26

Scanning below, I can just make out the long strands of Kain's hair.

"Kain, what are you doing over here? You'll be caught!"

"Shh. Anchor your hair on that pole. I'm coming up."

A thrill of excitement runs through me as I obey. I have no idea what is in store, but having a guest is worth the punishment.

My hair tightens as he tests its strength, but before I know it, Kain is stepping through my only portal to the outside world. Thinking I must be dreaming of having a wild, hot unicorn shifter in my rooms, I can't help but pinch myself.

"Are you alone?" Kain whispers as he drops down beside me.

"No, Wren and Altair are in the next room. If they catch you in here—"

Kain presses a finger on my lips, and my heart begins to beat even more furiously. Silently the unicorn raises my hair and motions for me to follow. When he gets to the guards' door, he pulls out a small vial from his pocket. With a wink in my direction, he pours a pink powder onto his hands and then blows it into the peephole.

"I traded some of my mane to the sprites that wait on the Queen. That will give us about four hours of peace," he says conspiratorially.

"You still didn't tell me how you got here," I admonish as we cross the room again.

Kain dips his finger into the frosting of my cake

and licks it off before his eyes lock on mine. My throat is suddenly dry; I watch as he takes the digit in his mouth to clean the rest of the sugary confection off. Fighting down the urge to join him, I fold my arms and give him my best impression of impatience.

"Oh yeah, the Queen is bedridden for the next month. She told the stables I could run the field at night to gather my strength. No doubt she wants me strong so she can break me again later, but no matter. As soon as I was out of sight, I made my way here. I thought maybe if I was lucky, we'd be able to exchange a few whispers but imagine my surprise when your hair fell down at my feet!"

It's hard not to join his enthusiasm when his lips are spread from ear to ear. Crossing the room, I slip a finger into the cake before stepping to his side. An air of anticipation hangs in the air as our eyes meet.

"What now?" I ask.

"We can do whatever you like," Kain smiles. "But first, let's bring your hair back in before anyone else gets the same idea as me."

With a chuckle, I help him pull in the long strands. Wishing I had a Fae maid to spell it into a shorter braid, I sigh and set to work trying to get it into a manageable pile. Kain dives in to help without even asking. Within moments, the two of us wrangle my golden locks into a large braid.

"How do you like your new freedom?" Kain takes a seat at the table.

"I've barely had time to enjoy it," I look around as if

seeing the small apartment for the first time. "I wonder what these rooms were used for before me?"

"You don't know?" Kain stands and steps into the moonlight beaming from the window.

"You do?" I question.

"I've been here a long time," Kain mutters. "I've seen more than I care to remember. And still less than I'd like, if that makes sense. Did you know that there's another Fae realm, and the Kingdom is all light Fae? None of the death and torture you find here."

"Wow. Honestly I don't know much about the world at all. I've been kept isolated my whole life, even before I was sold to Thayer," my voice catches as I remember the night I was brought here.

"What? Why?" Kain pulls me close to him.

Looking up at the starry sky, I shake my head. "I'm beginning to wonder that myself. Kain, I think my entire life has been a lie. Memories keep surfacing of a couple with crowns. The man looks just like me. I was raised by Gothel in a tower just beyond the border. She kept me hidden because of my hair, so she said. But what if I was never really hers?"

I turn and look into Kain's eyes. His brows furrow and he folds me in his arms. "Someday, I'll help you find those answers. I lost my family when I was only a foal. If I can help you find yours, I will."

"How did you lose your family?"

Kain opens his mouth to speak but stops short when we hear the unmistakable sound of the gates opening. "What the—?" Kain darts to the window. "There's rarely anyone allowed to enter at this hour."

Since I've lived most of my time in the cells, I have no clue about the gate schedule. With a shrug, I join the unicorn at the window. Once the gates open, a trio of Fae guards drags in a group of prisoners. This is nothing new, but the fact that two groups have been brought in, in two days is unusual.

"What kind of magical creatures do you think they brought?" Kain elbows me.

Scanning the small group, I put a finger to my lips. "Well, the first one is obviously a centaur. Has the Queen grown tired of you pulling her chariot?" I tease.

"Hmph," Kain winks. "I'd like nothing more, but then I'd be afraid of where she'd send me next. The other two are hatchling dragons. I'm sure they'll be raised to keep the fae smithery hotter than hell. But what about the one in the back?"

Smiling at our back and forth, I spot the last prisoner. He's tall, but not as tall as the Fae guards, with a princely mop of brown hair. The rest is hard to see in the torchlight. "Honestly, he looks unremarkable, almost human. He must be a shifter of some sort. Maybe a wolf. He looks a little wild."

As soon as I say that, the man stares toward my window. I take a step back, not wanting to be seen. What is it about these prisoners seeming to know where I am?

"No way to tell until they place him," Kain smiles and leads me to the table. "Can I have a piece of your cake?"

Blushing involuntarily, I busy myself grabbing plates. Serving up two slices, I sit next to Kain at the table and take my first bite. The sweet flavor bursts on my tongue, and I almost moan.

"This is delicious," Kain sighs. "Definitely worth climbing this crumbling tower."

"Oh? My company wasn't good enough?" I feign hurt feelings.

Setting his fork down, Kain places a hand over his heart. "Ouch. You know you're my obsession, Zelle. You can't be that oblivious."

For the second time this night, my heart pitter-patters. "I, uh."

"Shh, don't think about it," Kain leans over and presses his lips to mine. The kiss is soft and slow. He tastes of sugar and night air. After a moment of bliss, he pulls away and stares into my eyes.

"We've got to find a way out of here, Zelle. Someone as good and beautiful as you shouldn't be made to live as a slave."

"Nor should you," I breathe.

"Then it's settled. We'll escape together! He jumps from the table. But for now, I must go. The guards will be looking for me soon. I'll visit when I can," Kain presses his lips to mine once more.

A tear threatens, but I help him out of the window the same way he came in. The further away he travels, the more my heart breaks. "Yes, we shall leave this place," I vow softly.

Kain

I couldn't believe my luck. Not only did I get up to Zelle's tower, but I got to kiss her finally. There has always been a pull to be near her. Hell, I'm pretty sure she's half the reason I've let the Queen whip me so often. The Queen thinks she's in charge, but I could hold my tongue if I chose to, which would give her less reason to beat me. Since Zelle's arrival, it's been a game. If I get under her skin enough, I will be rewarded with a trip to see Zelle. The Queen has been none the wiser about my true motives.

With my head in the clouds, I slink into the shadows; I risked more than a beating to see Zelle tonight. If I got caught, there would be more than my head on the chopping block. Once I reach my usual running grounds, I let the shift from human to unicorn begin. Running as a human doesn't give me the excitement or feeling of freedom I get in my unicorn form.

As soon as my hooves begin to form, I set off into a run. The change always starts in my legs, they begin to change from feet to hooves, and my skin is replaced with a short white coat of hair. My rags rip away as the shift moves up my body. My back arches with the change. After all these years, it no longer hurts. It's nothing more than a dull ache that disappears the longer I run. Once my transformation is complete, I pick up the pace, my heart rate increasing and my blood pumping. The feeling I get as I race toward the border is hard to describe.

The pitfall of my run is the freedom for my mind to wander. Memories always take over from the night the Queen sent her army to kill my family. I was about seven, but that scene is etched in my soul as if it was yesterday.

"Kain, you must hide. No matter what you hear, do not come out until there are no voices. Promise me this," my mother said as tears streamed down her cheeks.

"I promise, mama," I squeaked as she pulled me in for one last hug.

"Never forget that your father and I love you to the stars and beyond," she squeezed me a little harder. "Never forget who you are and how strong you can be. We are proud of you and know that you will grow into a stallion we would be proud of."

She loosened her grip, "Now into the cabinet like we practiced."

I nodded and moved the food we had stored to help me hide. There was a booming sound as the front door of our castle slammed open.

My heart pounds, and I try to disappear into the shadows. The voice's echo yelled, "By decree of the

Queen of Wolgast, being a unicorn shifter is illegal. All must be slain."

Wincing, I plugged my ears to no avail, as my parents' screams still haunt me in my dreams today. The waiting seemed like days. The guards laughed as they left, boasting of how the fire was the best way to cleanse my family's lands. I knew I needed to leave the house but didn't dare move. That was until the flames began licking the cabinet doors. I bolted from my spot, only stopping to vow vengeance over my family's blood-soaked bodies.

The image of my mother's lifeless eyes spurs me out of the memory, and I notice that I'm near the border, but I don't stop. Instead, I veer towards the cells thinking maybe I can get a peek at the newbies that were brought in.

If I stay in my unicorn form, it will raise fewer eyebrows. As usual, the Fae guards assume I'm just a dumb horse with a horn and don't pay me much mind. So, I take full advantage of that and roam freely.

My sense of smell leads me to the tent where the slaves have been taken. Playing my part well, I let out a whinny when one of the guards catches sight of me. The guard pats my nose and moves on. Idiots. Making a nuisance, I trot over to the huddle of bodies. The new prisoner's eyes widen as I approach him, and a few guards swarm us.

"Back up, Kain," the closest one says, reaching up to pet my mane.

Inwardly I scowl, but I prance as if I love the attention. I hate letting the guard touch me, but if I want to keep the Fae in the dark of my shifting, I have to keep up appearances. Even the Queen is in the dark about my shifting ability. If she caught wind that I was the last of my kind, there's no telling what hell she'd rain down on me.

The guard continues scratching behind my ears, chuckling to himself. "This guy is not only wanted in the Fae realm but the Mortal realm as well. The Queen will be tickled to death that we caught this scumbag."

I neigh at his words, and he just laughs. "Off with you. Time to lock down for the night."

Trotting off, I head to the tree line, where I keep an extra set of clothes. Once I make it there, I start the change back. It takes less time to return to being human, and I dress just as fast. I want to speak with this new guy; my gut tells me he may be the key to getting Zelle and me out of here.

Staying in the shadows, I watch as the prisoners are brought to the cellblock. Once the guards leave, I approach the now quiet cell and head around toward the little window at the back.

"Psst," I whisper with my face as close to the opening as I dare.

"Hmm?" he mutters.

"What did you do to be welcomed with such fanfare?" I question, raising my voice just a bit.

"The list of what I haven't done may be shorter," he muses. "Maybe you've heard of me? I'm Flynn Rider, outlaw, and thief.

"Nope never heard of you. Charmed, I'm sure. I'm

Kain. Tell me, are you any good at escaping?" I ask, hope in my tone.

"Depends on what you have in mind. From this camp? This realm? Gotta narrow the options a little," he replies.

"Well, firstly, the camp. There's someone special here. I promised her freedom, and I plan to make good on my word," I confess, unsure why I told him.

"Her, huh? Are there many women here?" he asks with a hint of amusement in his tone.

"A few, but none like her," I answer. My belly does a flip as I remember the touch of her lips.

"Say I can help. First, I want to meet this special lady," he states, his voice growing louder as he nears the window.

I sigh, "With how they put you in lockdown, a beating will be the only way."

"A beating? Just to get face-to-face with your friend? That seems a little drastic," he comments.

"Well, like me, she is somewhat a pet for the King," I tell him, "But the Queen, on the other hand, is my keeper. I am her trained horse with a horn, and Zelle is the medic. So yes, injury is the only way to see her."

"That's interesting. Why should I believe you?" he questions.

I don't take offense to his question. If I was in his shoes, I might be suspicious as well.

"If they let you out of your cell tomorrow, ask around. You'll see I speak the truth," I say as I look around. Sunrise will be coming, and I'd best get back to my stall. Hoping the stranger would heed my words, I backed away from the window and ran into the bush to hide my clothing. Transforming quickly, I gallop away. *Goddess, let my instincts prove me right again.*

No matter the reason, my hooves hitting the sod is heavenly. Shaking my head, I take a deep draw of the damp night air as I glide across the field toward the Royal stables. Once I get within hearing distance, I slow to a canter and enter as if I own the place. The guards are used to my uppity behavior and open my stall with a groan. They know full well not to touch me. Only the Queen gets to abuse me.

There are a few benefits to being the Queen's pet. My stall is always clean, and I'm fed better than the other slaves besides Zelle. The King favors her for her healing, so she's treated with a little more kindness than our counterparts. I hate watching the other magical creatures being overworked and underfed, but there's nothing I can do to help.

There are two other unicorns and one pegasus in the stable. I mostly keep to myself as I'm the only male and the females are persnickety. Plus, my equine-speak is horrid. I understand fine—it's just that I was too young when my parents were taken to remember how to communicate while on hooves. In our kingdom, foals cannot shift until they hit puberty. Just my luck that I was caught by King Thayer months after puberty. I had gotten quite good at hiding as a human but was enjoying a nice gallop when his spies caught sight of me.

Honestly, until Zelle came, I didn't mind being a slave. The Queen feeds me well and only mistreats me when I act a fool—which lately is a lot. I can't help myself. Knowing Zelle will wrap her hair around me afterward makes me want to be bad. Maybe I'm a masochist?

"Quiet down in there, Kain!" Durin, my handler bangs on the stall.

Chuffing in reply, I settle into my hay. I hadn't realized I was making any noise. My nostrils flare as I try and fail to get my mind off the things I'd like Zelle to do to me. Fuck! Will she love me when she finds out about my baser nature? I guess only time will tell.

❋

Morning comes swiftly. The stables come alive with noises as the handlers come in and open each stall. Breakfast is always served before we're groomed and led to stand before the Queen. Although with her on bedrest, who knows what today might bring.

'I heard the Queen was with child,' Star leans her head over my stall. 'Is that why they let you roll in human scent last night?' The older unicorn sniffs the air.

'Good. I like human stink,' I move to the other side of my space. It's a mystery to me that these three haven't figured out why I so often come back smelling like a person.

The mare rolls her eyes before leaving my sight. I guess if I tried, I could communicate, but honestly I don't like my roommates enough to find out.

"Breakfast," Durin's round face appears as the gate opens. The handlers are all Dwarves, which has always struck me as odd since they're so short but at least they're nicer than the Fae.

With a small nicker, I edge out of my stall and enter the larger stable. Fresh grains have been set in the trough along with apple slices. Stomach roaring, I find a spot and dig into the meal wholeheartedly. Human food is great, but grains go down easier and don't make me feel heavy.

'Why can't you eat without slobbering in the trough?' Diamond nips at my shoulder.

With a horse-grin, I move to the side and dig my nose down into the pile of grain just to get her riled up. It works beautifully. Diamond lets out a neigh as she flaps her white wings and stomps a hoof at me, letting loose a few feathers in her efforts. Chuckling inside, I take a few more mouthfuls before I leave the trough, head held high.

'Why I never," Luna glares at me as I pass. She's the only one near my age. I'd say ten years older than my fifty whereas the other two are at least a hundred.

Happy with my mischief, I trot over to Durin who is waiting with a brush. This is my favorite part of being in my equine form. Grooming is pure heaven if it's done right, and my handler is the best.

A few strokes in, my eyes roll back in my head. The ecstasy is broken when a loud metal clang reverberates through the stables. Startled, I perk my ears up and swing my head in the direction of the sound. What I see sends a ripple of fear down my back.

"Fire! The stable is burning, get the animals out!" a voice yells.

Durin throws down the brush and mounts me before I can think. With a quick yank to my mane, he steers us toward the exit. Fear overtakes me and my vision blurs as we race through the rows of hay. Rays of sunlight beckon me forward but out of nowhere a flaming beam falls into my path. Bucking Durin off, I charge forward to no avail. Another beam crashes down on my back, nailing me to the ground.

"Get the Queen's favorite before we lose our heads!" are the last words I hear before darkness overtakes me.

Zelle

"Zelle, there's an emergency at the stalls. We're going to use the normal exit. Hurry now, girl, before the Queen's favorite steed is lost."

Foggy-headed, I stumble to obey. I can tell Altair is alone by the friendly tone he uses. Wondering where Wren was and why I was being rushed, I glanced in the guard's direction.

Fear slices my heart. Kain. Moving faster, I slip on a dress over my nightgown and cross the room as I grab my shoes. "I'm ready."

Altair smiles faintly, then takes my arm. He doesn't bother to blindfold me as he brings me into the guard room. I'm hit with the musky, male scent as we cross the pristine living quarters and approach a wooden door. Altair opens the door revealing a winding staircase made of stone. His hand still gripping me, and the guard rushes down the spiral. His momentum all but drags me, but I don't care.

A lump forms in my throat as I prepare for what I'm about to see. Knowing the Queen, there's no telling what state Kain will be in when we arrive.

I knew if it wasn't for the weight of my hair, Altair would carry me because I was slowing them down. At least I could see, although I still find myself tripping blindfold or not. As soon as we hit the landing, Wren plows through the door, almost knocking it off its hinges. That's when the scent of ash fills my nose, and my heart sinks.

How was there a fire at the stables? I try to keep the tears at bay. No one can know about my feelings for Kain. I certainly can't be a blubbering mess when I arrive. Out of all the injuries I heal, burns tend to be the hardest. Magic is tricky like that. Yes, I could care for them, but the pain of wrapping my hair near or on a burn turns my stomach.

I say a silent prayer to anyone or anything who might be listening, hoping that Kain will survive. Did the fates conspire against us? The morning after he promised we would escape, the stable went up in flames. There's no way it's dumb luck.

My heart stops the moment the barns come into sight. There are still some flames licking at the wooden structure. *Oh my sweet, Kain, you can't leave me.*

We only slow once we are mere feet from the stable doors. Altair's grip eases as we stop, "You will say right here. Anyone hurt will be brought to you. Do you understand, Zelle?"

There is a lump in my throat, my mouth too dry to speak, so all I can do is nod.

"Right here," Altair states as he points toward my feet.

"Yes, Altair," I finally manage.

I watch the guards move closer to the burning building but don't enter. This was the first time since my mother sold me to the King that I felt helpless. I wrap my arms around myself as I stand there like a bump on a log.

Could I do anything? If my hair caught fire, it would end my usefulness, and part of me likes the idea. Until I realize that if Kain is hurt, I wouldn't be able to fix him. Once more, I'd be thrown in the labor block with the other humans, no longer a valued prize.

My thoughts are interrupted when a gruff voice yells, "Move, Angel. Into the barn! Get in there and help pull out the remaining corpses. The Queen will see they are given a proper burial!" The Fae guard shoves Xavier.

Xavier glances in my direction. We lock eyes for a moment then he winks before heading into the stables.

I can't breathe. The thought of either man perishing almost has me hyperventilating. Needing to do something with my hands, I unbraid my hair, which always seems to soothe me. It is my one constant in this hell hole, and I can use it to do good. I don't realize that I'm humming as I work until the golden locks glow. The guard that brought Xavier's jaw snaps open.

"Zelle, hurry, they have found two survivors," Altair yells from just outside of the stable entrance.

Please be Kain, please be Kain, I repeat as I jog over to where Altair and Wren stand. Wren has been too quiet this morning. He loves to yell at me. I don't have time to think about that as Xavier reappears. Smoke bellows out, blocking my view of him until he steps into the clear with a dwarf in one hand and a soot-covered unicorn thrown over his shoulder like a sack of potatoes. Kain.

"Where do you wish for these two to lie?" Xavier questions.

I run an eye over the two in his hands, and it's easier to breathe as I note the rise and fall of their chests.

"Next to Zelle," Wren orders, pointing but not looking at me.

Xavier doesn't wait for another order. He closes the distance between us. With careful hands, he lays them on either side of me.

"How can I help you, Zelle?" the Fallen Angel asks.

"Help me wrap my hair around the dwarf. I'll get this unicorn," I tell him.

He nods, gathers a section of my hair, and encases the tiny man within the strands. I do the same with Kain. The tears don't stay at bay this time, and I don't bother to hide them. Xavier takes a step back once he completes his task, and I'm almost done as I start my song.

The tears still flow as I sing. Thankfully, my magic responds quickly, and the glow moves down my hair and over the two men in my care. Smoke inhalation is not something I have treated, so I don't know if this will work. But they start to choke and wiggle within moments, both good signs. The dwarf starts trying to release himself at the same time that Kain tries to rise.

"You need to hold them down," I say to the guards just staring at me. Wren has his typical look of distaste but jumps to help Altair with Kain.

"Someone needs to hold the dwarf."

Xavier places his hand on the tiny man's forehead and mutters, "Rest." The dwarf stills.

Apparently, he still possesses some of his former powers, as fallen as he might be. Good to know. My head spins in a thousand different directions. Maybe I can convince Kain we should let the Angel tag along when we escape.

Stop it, Zelle. Heal Kain, then plan your escape, I chide myself.

"Zelle, are you healing them or making it worse?" Wren complains.

"Trust the process. It has yet to fail me," I promise, wiping the wetness from my eyes.

The tears have come to a stop, at least for now. After a few more grueling minutes, the dwarf's eyes flutter open.

"Altair, you can unwrap the dwarf?" I ask as I begin to panic. Kain will need to shift before I can fully heal him, and he can't do that here.

"Xavier, I need you to carry Kain to my cell. I can't heal him properly here," I command, hoping the Fae don't question my motives. His eyes grow wide as he looks from the unicorn to my tear-streaked face. "Yes, of course. Lead the way."

"Zelle?" Wren stares.

"Please. Kain won't last much longer out in the open with these wounds," I beg.

"Fine. But go straight to the cell, or you will both be punished."

With a nod, I turn toward the prison. The stone

building looms over the courtyard like a dark stain. The guard barely looks at us at the entrance before opening the gate. He knows where we're headed without asking. Thank the stars for small miracles.

The hall is quiet. Only the drip of water marks our passage. After what feels like hours, we approach my old cell. I pass the doorway and point for Xavier to enter first.

"Lay him on the floor," I state as I close the door as much as I dare. "You can't tell anyone what you're about to see," I whisper as I kneel at Kain's head.

Xavier raises an eyebrow and crosses his arms. "You barely know me, and you're calling me a snitch?"

Wrinkling my nose, I pet Kain's cheek. Obviously, Xavier will hold our secret. "Shh. Kain, you'll need to shift now," I whisper, a tear falling onto his nose.

"Lay as much of my hair over him as you can." I look up to the angel.

He moves faster than I'd expected, cascading my locks over the unicorn. Humming softly, I continue my vigil. Kain's body shivers and then begins to morph. A bright white light surrounds him before his body blinks out of existence for a moment. I close my eyes, praying to the stars. When I open my eyes again, Kain's human eyes lock with mine.

"Zelle?"

"Rest and don't move just yet. Do you know where you are?" I question.

"Yes, I know this room. What about the stables?" he mutters, "Everyone get out?"

Before I can answer, Xavier says, "Yes, you and the small one were the only ones left inside."

Kain gives him a little nod before closing his eyes again. We sit in silence for what feels like an eternity. I alternate singing and resting while Xavier keeps the guards from entering the cell. At one point, he walks down the hall, talking to Wren. I'd wonder why we've been given so much levity if I didn't know how obsessive the Queen could be over her toys.

"You need to eat," Xavier reappears and I smell the biscuits before he reveals them.

Every fiber of my being can taste the warm bread before I have it in my hands. Xavier hands one over with a smirk and watches as I take the first bite. Part of me wants to gobble it down like a beast, but I don't. Instead, I take a huge bite and savor it as I chew.

"Easy there chipmunk," Xavier laughs. "How's the horny dude?"

Unperturbed by the slight, I take another big bite and enjoy it to the fullest before answering. "He should wake any minute I think, hard to tell really."

"Are those crumbs dropping in my face?" Kain shakes his head.

Oops. Cheeks ablaze, I dust the rest out of his hair. "Welcome back! How are you feeling?"

Kain closes his eyes for a moment before looking up at me. "Nothing hurts, but your hair tickles. Unless you want to see what I'm working with I need the robe."

"Right," I almost die. "Xavier, can you grab the robe off the wall?" I point.

Xavier crosses the room with the robe and helps Kain up while I keep my eyes focused on the ceiling. I certainly did not sneak a peek of Kain's sculpted ass in the process, nope not me. Itching to get up, I spring to my feet and pace before the doorway.

"Thanks for saving me, angel," Kain says before I feel his arms snake around my waist. "And thank you for the second healing this week."

My stomach in knots, I sigh and relax into his arms for a brief moment.

"I hate to cut this short," Xavier clears his throat. "But those guards are not going to stay away forever."

"True. You'd better shift back, Kain," I whisper.

"Right. No doubt I'll be in the cell block this evening. Xavier is it? I'll find you and we'll sneak over to Zelle. See you later!" Kain shifts before either of us can argue.

"Do not do anything that will get either of you in trouble," I take him by the mane and lead him out the door. "Wren? Altair?" I call.

Both guards jump from their chairs.

"Nice work. The Queen will be pleased," Wren says gruffly. "I'll take the unicorn to see her if you'll bring the human back to her rooms?" Wren asks Altair.

"First I have to find a place for the angel," Altair grumbles.

"Eh, just leave him in the girl's old cell. We'll deal with him later," Wren throws a rope over Kain's head and leaves.

Zelle

Wren leads Kain away quickly and I feel as if he's taking a piece of my heart with him. I've healed him at least once a week since I arrived in this kingdom. In those small moments, we've shared secrets and enjoyed what small amounts of each other's time that we could. Him stealing into my room and kissing me has made the bond all that more strong.

"Walk with me," Altair waves his hand in my face. Unlike Wren, he hardly ever lays a hand on me.

When we reach my old cell, Xavier is sitting on the bed, one elbow propped on his knee to hold his head. His wings are spread out so that they take up most of the space around the small bed.

"Zelle, go fetch the water pail from the end of the hall," Altair orders.

Without a second thought, I turn down the dead-end corridor and trek toward the running well at the end. My head is a jumble of mixed-up emotions when I hear a voice singing quietly.

"Odd, I've never seen anyone at this end of the prison," I whisper.

Taking two steps forward, I peer into the last cell. Hidden in the corner is a being with long, gray hair. The green blanket wrapped around its body all but hides anything but the silver strands that reach the ground.

"Hello?" I touch the bars separating us.

The singing stops and a silence grows between us. "Are you okay?"

The head turns and a wrinkled face appears. Ever so slowly, the eyes blink and take me in. "I knew you'd find me before my time ran out," the melodic voice is so low I have to strain to hear her.

"Do I know you?"

"No, but I know of you, sweet girl. Your magic calls to me, reminds me of what I once was. Before I was taken and so was my spirit. I've been saving the last of my charms to gift to one such as yourself. I was once a Goddess of Vengeance. I have many names and forms, but you may call me Prax. Those who worshiped me have long gone, there is no need to use my full name."

"A Goddess?" I inhale. "How is it that they've kept you here?"

"Oh that is a tale that is meant to be told with more time than you have. Find your way back to me in a fortnight. You will need three by your side who are trustworthy. Only when you are ready to embark on this quest of vengeance should you return. Now go!" Prax's voice thunders in my ears and the cell goes dark. Try as I might, I can no longer see beyond the bars.

Trembling, I set off toward the water Altair sent me

to fetch and hurry back to the cell where he and Xavier await.

"Did you forget the way?" Altair grumbles and points toward the foot of the bed.

Not daring to try and speak, I shake my head and set the bucket down.

"Rest, angel, your duties in the palace will begin tomorrow. Food will be brought after the first bell tolls," Altair motions for me to exit and then closes the cell behind us, charming the door.

Feeling as if I might implode, I follow the guard almost mechanically out of the prison and back to the tower. He doesn't bother with the annoying bucket, which is a small relief. We make our way up the winding staircase in the dark, no words spoken.

"Wren will be up soon enough, hurry to your quarters and get in bed," Altair shoos me out of the guard room.

Not wanting to chance Wren's wrath, I do as I'm told. Once I'm in the bed, I lay listening for signs that Kain has come. Pascal peeks over the headboard, then settles on the pillow next to me. Hours go by with nothing stirring but the wind. Exhausted, I close my eyes. Kain must not have been able to escape this night.

❋

The door to my quarters is thrown open, waking me from a restful sleep.

"Time to get moving, Zelle!" Wren yells

from the doorway. "You have five minutes to get your butt dressed and ready."

I throw back the covers and hop to it, knowing that if I test their patience I won't get to check on Kain or Xavier. I slip off the nightgown and trade it for the modest purple and pink dress in the chest.

Doing my best, I tame my flowing locks, cursing myself for not braiding them back last night.

"Two minutes," Wren yells his warning.

I don't answer, just move faster, if I've learned one thing here it's not to reply. Wren sees it as backtalk and that just leaves me with a beating and bruising. Too many nights nursing my wounds, too proud to heal myself, seeing my guards wince when they note the damage that they have done to me.

I'm slipping on my shoes as Wren enters my room. "Time's up, doll. Let's get moving."

'Doll?' Did he just call me that? That's so unlike him, but I just shake it off to exhaustion from the night's events.

"I'm ready," I say as I move toward the door that joins our rooms. I spot Altair and he just gives me a shrug.

"It's about time," Altair says flatly as he heads toward the staircase.

"Get moving," Wren orders as he motions to the staircase.

I nod and do as he says. I remind myself that I'm still a prisoner here and always will be. That any kindness I'm shown is only because I'm useful. If I want to stay in their good graces, until I can escape, I must comply.

Altair starts down the stairs ahead of me with Wren bringing up the rear. The only sound audible is the thumping of our feet on the steps. I'm grateful for the sun on my face as Altair opens the door in front of us.

The butterflies in my stomach flutter more and more as we near the cells. The thought of seeing Xavier has me on edge mixed with some excitement and some hopefulness. He didn't look well when we left but I didn't have a choice in the matter.

I'm holding my breath until Altair unlocks the cell door and that beautiful fallen angel is there waiting for me.

"Do your thing and we will get him out of here so you both can work," Wren orders.

I do my best to pull my hair down and wrap it around the protesting angel. He's much more melancholy than yesterday.

Stopping in front of him, I plead, "Xavier, please let me heal you. I don't know why but I will need you for what is to come."

His gaze snaps up to mine and he nods in approval.

Once I'm satisfied he is covered enough, I start my song and my hair starts to glow.

As my words end, Wren is in the cell, pulling my hair from around the Fallen Angel and yanking me to the side. Altair locks the cell once more before grunting at Wren.

"This is no longer your work room, the injured will

be brought to you," my jailer informs me as we make our way back to the tower.

I don't understand why they took me out of the tower just to take me back, but it will be a nice change to be free of that small, musty place.

To my annoyance, they make me take the bucket back up, Altair going first. The squeak of the wheel that houses the rope will haunt me in my dreams.

I wash my hands before I take a seat and wait on the next victim of the queen's abuse, when a handsome man with a smolder on his face, jumps out of the bucket. Could this be the troublemaker that had the caravan of guards the other night? I could see that it would be him.

"Be careful with this one, his hands are just as slick as his tongue," Altair warns.

Not sure what he means, I eye the man carefully. "What can I heal for you today?"

He winks at me, before whispering, "Kain sent me."

I'm a little taken aback at his words. How can that be? Kain only came to be healed in his unicorn form, he didn't want the queen to know what he truly was.

"Where are you hurt?" I ask as I glance toward the guards.

"Will you be okay with this one?" Wren asks as he steps closer to us.

"Yes, sir. I'm just looking over him in preparation to heal his injuries," I reply.

"Altair and I will be in the other room if you need us, but the door will be open," Wren states as he walks toward the tiny guard room.

"Thank you, sir," I say as he leaves me with the stranger. "They warn me against you, and then leave me alone in a room with you." I pinch my lips at the stranger.

I don't understand these men.

"So, what are you here for?" I ask.

"I have a cut on my thigh," he smiles as he unhooks the belt of his pants.

I avert my eyes just as he pulls them down and grab a towel from the cupboard. "Use this to cover up," I tell him, thrusting the fabric towards him.

"Shy, I see," he states with laughter in his tone.

"It wouldn't hurt you to have some modesty," I complain.

"I'm decent," he sighs.

I open my eyes and sigh with relief when I note the towel is covering all of the important stuff. His inner thigh is punctured, maybe all the way through. Tough to tell with all the blood seeping out..

"How did this happen?" I ask, as I bend and attempt to wrap my hair around the appendage.

"Whoa. First tell me why you're putting your hair on my wound." He jumps back, raising an eyebrow.

This time, I'm the one to clap back, "Magic hair."

"What? Magic hair? I don't believe it," he states.

"You were kidnapped by Fae and are surrounded by magical creatures but you don't believe I have magic hair?" I put a hand on my hip. Did you say that Kain sent you?" I ask, changing the subject.

"Yes, he said you two want out of here and he thinks I'm the key," he smiles, almost blinding me with his white teeth. "So, I let him slash me with his horn for a ticket to the tower."

"I see." I bite back a smartass retort. "Are you planning on telling me who you are that would make Kain say that?"

The look he gives almost melts me on the spot. Which is totally unfair. "You can call me Flynn. I'm sort of a bounty hunter or thief. Whichever gets me what I want at the moment. I was on the hunt for the lost princess of Corona when I got snatched," he finished with a weird look on his face.

"Never heard of it, or you," I dismiss, forcing my hair around his thigh so I can get this over with. My fingers graze a little higher than I'd intended and Flynn freezes.

Not wanting to make a bigger deal than I already have, I begin my incantation. Flynn stands still as a rock while the strands glow and do their thing. In no time, he's back to normal and I begin unwinding my hair.

"If Kain thinks you can help, I trust him. But that doesn't mean I trust you—yet," I peer up at the unforgettably handsome man.

Flynn looks down at me as if he's about to speak, but then his eyes scan the spot that was moments ago a gory mess. "Holy shit!" He jumps up, knocking the towel off and flopping his bits and pieces everywhere.

In shock, I can't help but stare. His dick looks different than I'd imagined one would look like, and it takes everything I have not to just reach out to touch it. In a moment of electric awkwardness his one-eye and me have a moment. Then the reality of the situation kicks in and I fall backwards, kicking my skirt up unceremoniously.

"I guess one good turn deserves another," Flynn laughs as he steals a peek before grabbing the towel to cover himself.

All I can do is brush down my skirt and laugh. Of course, the first dick I see would be one that's flapping in front of my face.

Zelle

Prax did say I'd need three by my side, maybe I should hear Flynn out. At the very least, his company is better than none. Ever since my birthday, I've felt an itch for change. Not that I've ever loved being a slave, but being locked away is familiar to me. No more, now it feels as if this very tower might crumble and leave me suffocating under its heavy stones.

"Do you think you can really help us leave?" I lean forward and whisper.

"I've gotten out of worse." Flynn winks and makes a circular motion with his finger. Realizing he means to get dressed, I turn my back toward him.

"Okay, I think you're all done," I say loud enough for the guards to hear. When I turn back, I nod. Hopefully, Kain will find a way to come back so that we can talk in private.

The red door opens a little wider and Altair steps into the room. "Come with me," he motions for Flynn to board the bucket. Flynn wrinkles his nose, but complies. For all he knows, that's the only way up to my room. The Fae love their mind games.

"Thanks, blondie," Flynn smirks as he's lowered out of my line of sight.

"Ooh!" I grimace. Males are so impossible, no matter their kind. Speaking of kind, I still don't know what Flynn could be. Weird as it may be, I can sort of feel magic when I'm healing and I did detect a small amount in Flynn. It was too small for him to be a shifter as I once thought, Kain's magic is big and feels heavy when I heal him. It's almost like a barrier that I have to cross in order to fix anything. Interesting, indeed.

Worn out from the last few days, I slump in a chair at the table. Lucky for me, no one else is brought up.

❋

I am rudely awakened with a tongue to the face from my new little green friend, Pascal.

"What was that for?" I question him as I use the fabric of my skirt to wipe the liquid from my face. Then my stomach rumbles and I hear a similar sound from the Chamaeleon.

"I suppose it is time to eat," I tell him as I rise from the chair and head into the little kitchen space. There were some fresh veggies in the cabinet that weren't there before. My guards must have brought them while I was snoring. "We have some vegetables and lettuce, what if I fix us a little salad? We also have a little left-over cake for a mini dessert."

Pascal nods his little head as if he is okay with this choice. I hum as I work and my tiny friend squeaks along with me. I chop in rhythm with my song, it helps to pass the time as my hunger grows.

"There," I set the knife down and gather the bowls needed. What time is it? I don't think that the Queen would let me waste the day away snoring. There has to be more to heal today. "Would you like to sit at the table with me?"

I glance at Pascal. He gives me a little nod of approval and I have to stifle a laugh. Bending, I scoop him up before setting both bowls on the little, round dining table. Before I sit, I also grab the leftover cake. I'll eat my salad first, but Pascal may want dessert before veggies and I am not one to judge.

Just as I raise my fork to my mouth, the whine of the bucket fills the room. Did I jinx myself when I thought the day had been too easy? With a groan, I stuff a large bite into my mouth, watching to see who will pop into the tower first. Wren appears swearing under his breath as he waits for the bucket to return.

It seems it's taking longer than normal to load the next prisoner, when Altair calls up. "This isn't going to work, bring her down."

Wren doesn't say anything, just turns toward me. Not needing instructions I rise from the table, ready to join him. I don't question him as he grabs my wrist and leads me down the tower stairs. When we make it to the spot Altair is standing, my beautiful unicorn is sprawled out on his side with labored breathing.

"What is wrong with him?" This time I do speak, not fearing retaliation.

"He was pulling the queen's carriage when he collapsed. We aren't healers, you tell us what's going on with him," Wren's voice has a familiar tinge of hatred.

I sigh, after all these years, do they really not know anything? My hair is magic and it heals. That doesn't mean I know anything about diagnosing the wounded. Days like today, I long for Fae scrolls or books on healing, but that's one thing they haven't gifted me.

"Your raised voice is making him anxious, can you please back away from us?" I ask, trying to keep the annoyance out of my tone.

They don't reply, of course, but do as I ask. I watch as they go to stand near the fences and watch as some of the prisoners work in the gardens.

"Kain, what have you done now?" I question as I run a hand down his mane.

He nuzzles into my hand as it reaches his cheek.

"You really have to stop hurting yourself just to come see me," I tell him.

He gives me a little neigh as if he is arguing.

"Don't give me that sass. It's not that I don't want to see you, but don't you know that it breaks my heart to see you hurt?" I ask him, in a low voice.

I glance from him to the guards and note that they have moved out of sight, below the fence line. At this angle, it should be safe for Kain to shift without their prying eyes. I remove my apron and lay it over where his manly pieces would be before telling him to shift.

He gives me a little nod and it begins. This is the first time I've dared to watch the change and the magic of it strikes me in awe.

"Be honest, which form do you prefer, man or unicorn?" he asks with a smirk on his lips.

"Unicorn," I say flatly and watch his face fall. "That one doesn't give me as much lip."

His smile returns as he realizes that I was teasing him.

"They will return to check on us soon, can you tell me why you collapsed?" I question, in a rush.

"I think it's just leftovers from the barn fire, my lungs feel as if they are heavy and that makes it hard to breathe," he replies.

"Okay, I'm going to wrap my hair around your chest, once you start to feel normal again, shift back," I tell him as I start to cover his middle.

"Did you see Flynn?" he asks in my ear as I get close.

"I did, do you really think we can trust him?" I question.

"I think that he boasts a little but yes. I promised you that I would get you out of here, didn't I?"

"That you did, I may have found someone else to help as well," I whisper.

"Oh?" he perks up.

"Bring the fallen angel and thief to get me out of the tower tonight. We have someone to visit in the cells," is all I tell him as I start with my song. When I'm finished, I back away from him. There is a smile on his face as he returns to his horned form.

"Don't let me down. The three of you need to be here tonight." I scratch his ear before whistling to the guards.

Kain nickers before trotting toward Wren. The guard seems surprised, but takes him by the lead and walks him away from the tower, leaving me standing alone in blessed silence. Taken aback, I scan the grounds, hoping to map my way from the tower to the prison in case the boys never show. I know Prax said I needed them, but maybe they need me.

"Back to your rooms with ya," Altair appears, waving his hand toward the side door.

Relieved to forgo the bucket once again, I hurry to the entrance. Who knows, maybe things are changing for the better around here. It seems ever since the Queen has been ill, my guards have been more lax.

"You're to have the rest of the day off," Altair mentions as we cross his room into mine.

"Okay. Thank you?" I turn, tilting my head.

"It's not me who made the decision. The King has stalled your healings for two days. He wants you to hold your strength before you're summoned to see the Queen."

My eyes widen with surprise and I gulp down the lump of fear that threatens to escape my mouth in a scream. I've never been called to the palace. The Queen's need must be great. What if I can't fix her? There have been a few prisoners that were beyond my help. In their case, there was no consequence, but the Queen?

"Rest. Eat. Hope that you live through the summoning," Altair bows slightly before turning and closing the door that separates our quarters.

My heart threatens to leap out of my chest as I make my way to the window bench.

"Pascal?" I wheeze in need of company.

Little feet skitter across the floor. My skirt tugs as my friend climbs up and finds a spot to rest on my shoulder. "Zelle," Pascal whispers in my ear.

Startled, I jump. "Pascal? You've been able to speak all this time?" I almost cry.

"I've been rolling in Fae dust since we met. It has not been an easy feat," he puts his little hands in the air and I almost fall into hysterics.

"I'm thankful, little friend," I nuzzle his head.

"I will smuggle dust in for you. Tonight you will meet your guardian and the guards must sleep," Pascal pats my shoulder.

"You've met her?" I side-eye the chameleon.

"I am small. I travel in all places," he nods.

"Well excuse me for not knowing you were attuned, I sigh. I guess I should have known better to think any creature is simple on this side of the border.

Pacal smiles and jumps off my shoulder onto the windowsill. "I will be back," he states before disappearing.

There's nothing left for me to do besides eat and tidy my space. I throw myself into baking bread, the one comfort I've craved since my enslavement. Mixing and kneading the dough brings me some peace. Before long, the smell of fresh bread fills the air. Practically salivating, I take it from the oven and place it on the window ledge.

Birds chirp as the sun dips below the horizon. I watch the sky near the border with it,

scanning the purple haze and hoping to someday cross over. I'd give anything for even a night in my old tower. At least there I had the illusion of freedom. Slavery is an emotional sickness that slowly chips away at your spirit. I don't know how much more I can take.

I wonder if my real parents are out there, waiting for me to come home. Something tells me that they are. There's nothing motherly about Gothel. The more I think about it, the more I'm sure I don't belong to her anymore than I belong to King Thayer.

"What if they've given up on me?" I whisper.

A sadness wraps around me, threatening my sanity. Then, out of nowhere I see a single lantern floating in the ever-darkening sky. It's the same kind that I see on my birthday. It seems to wave at me, beckoning me to follow.

"Please be out there." I close my eyes and wish on the stars.

"Your wish is my command," a voice whispers below. "Zelle, let down your hair."

It is Kain, he didn't forget to come see me.

"One minute, let me check on the door to the guards' room," I whisper down. I run across the small space and note that it is closed before returning to the window. "Let me unbraid some and I'll throw it down."

"Make it fast, I don't like hanging out down here," Kain calls back up.

My fingers fumble to get the ends loose, grateful that Kain isn't here to watch me fail. I do this day in and out and now is the time my hands fail me?

"Almost there," I say, not sure if I'm reassuring Kain or myself.

Finally, I make some progress, enough that I can send it down to my unicorn shifter at least.

I watch as far as I can see it drop down into the darkness. There is a slight tug, telling me that Kain is starting his ascent. I'm almost giddy at seeing him. I'm not used to spending the day in my tower. Back in my cell I was able to converse with the others, walls between us or not.

"Rough day?" Kain smirks as he jumps in the window.

"Nah, just long. I've been ordered to rest as I'm to be called on by the Queen soon to heal her. Makes me wonder what is going on with her even more," I confess.

"Rumors have been floating around the prisoners that she is sick or with child. I've even heard a few whispers that she is dying," Kain informs me.

"Well, I can heal the hurt and ailing but I've never been tasked in healing the dying," I tell him as I start to rebraid my hair.

"If you put your hair back in the ties, how am I to escape back into the night?" He smiles.

"Oh, sorry. Will the others be here soon?" I ask, bouncing a foot, my nerves getting the best of me.

"Flynn agreed to come, but your angel may be a different story. He is a hard one to read," Kain states.

"Prax said to bring three, I don't think she has much time left. Should we go down to meet them?" I question.

"What if you wait here, let me head down and check? If one of the guards is patrolling, we can't let you get caught," he reminds me.

"I don't like the idea of you getting captured. I need all of you to come with me to see Prax, and I'm not sure what they will do to you if you are caught near my tower. Would they know you in this form?" I ask, pointing toward his human shape.

"There are only two people here that have seen me like this. You and Flynn," he admits.

"How did you talk to Xavier then?" I query.

"Flynn, he did all the talking. I think he likes the sound of his own voice. He would talk to a tree just to hear himself," Kain jokes.

"He does have a nice voice," I admit.

"Oh no, does he have you under his spell, too?" Kain puts a palm on his head in mock disdain.

"Spell?" I ask. "I'm not sure what you mean."

"Never mind that now, let down your hair and I'll check for the others," Kain orders.

I move toward the window and throw my hair down into the blackness. As I turn, Kain gives me a peck on the lips before descending into the abyss. Once at the bottom he gives it a little tug and I pull my hair up so he can check for not only the others but the guards as well.

I send a silent prayer out that he doesn't get snatched but I must have been too late as a voice yells, "What the hell are you doing here?"

I know that voice, it's Altair. My blood runs cold when he hollers, "Looks like you get to visit our King."

I'm leaning on the window sill, my nails digging into the wood when Wren bursts into my room. I jump at the noise and turn to face him. "What is the meaning of this?"

"There was a prisoner lurking at the base of the tower, I had to make sure that there wasn't another in here with you," he says.

"How on Earth would anyone get in here with me?" I question, raising my tone a little. "Do you think that I'm stupid enough to jeopardize this little slice of freedom for a late night visit?"

"Uh. I don't know. No! I just feared for your safety," he backpedals toward the door.

"Oh," I mutter, "Then I apologize for my rudeness. I heard the commotion outside and you charged in, setting me on edge."

"Think no more of it, there are only two ways up. Altair removes the bucket at night and not many know about the other entrance. I suggest you get to bed and rest."

"Thank you for your kindness, Wren. I think I will head to bed," I say with a little smile.

I know he's only doing his job, but he doesn't seem as gruff here as of late. Maybe I'm more tired than I realized. I fear for Kain and what will happen to him, but now I know we can't go visit Prax tonight. A tear rolls down my cheek as I make it over to the bed as Wren leaves, closing the door behind him. I'm stuck here yet again.

Kain

It figures as soon as my feet touch the ground, Altair would appear. Now I'm scrambling to try and come up with an alternate identity as he marches me toward the palace. I know better than to prance around without sniffing the air. Being with Zelle got me too distracted, and now I'll pay for my transgression in carelessness.

"You might want to think about what you'll say to the King when we arrive. He won't be happy to have a straggler about at night," the guard pokes me with a spear.

Sweat breaks out on my forehead as my mind spins in circles. If they find out I'm a unicorn shifter, my life will be over. If I'm lucky it will be a swift death, but that's not likely.

"Altair, who's that?" the palace guard calls out as we approach the entrance.

"That's a good question, Fenix. I caught him wandering the grounds near my charge's tower."

Fenix scratches his chin, but opens the door for us. A wisp of cool air greets us as we step over the white marble threshold. Everything in the palace is white or gold. Not very Fae-like if you ask me, but what do I know?

Altair's boots squeak as we walk the long hallway. Try as I might, I can't think of a plausible story to tell the King. My stomach begins to knot and I gulp back the bile that rises.

"Altair, you must be crazy to darken the King's quarters at this hour!" a maid states as she exits one of the Queen's rooms. The air that follows her tastes coppery and stale. She stops, wiping her hands on her apron. "He's with the Queen, and shouldn't be disturbed. Can't you handle this prisoner on your own?"

"Aye, I suppose I could lock him up in the viewing room. Will you send a message to King Thayer to call for me in the morning to deal with the situation?"

The maid curtseys and gives Altair a nod. "Smart choice. I'll let him know once I return." And then she disappears around the next corner.

"Good news for you," Altair grumbles. "The viewing room is where the Queen keeps her pets, so it's a little more comfortable than the prison. But don't get any ideas, the security here is far superior." He almost laughs.

I grimace, knowing full well what the viewing room is like. I've spent more time in that padded room than I care to count. If only I'd been more careful, I could be with Zelle right now, but I'm a dumbass.

The all-too-familiar scent of the viewing room hits me two paces before we step to the door. Altair drags me inside and before I know it, I'm in a gilded cage. The only light is the scant ray beaming in from the hallway, but I already know the details of this room. This cage housed a phoenix for a time, as I recall with unease. Her feathers still litter the floor. I wasn't around when she was slain, and for that small grace I'm thankful. For the rebirthing bird to be gone, it must have been gruesome.

The lock clicks and Altair gives me a sad smile. "Rest before your questioning. There's no quarter given to wrong-doers in this Kingdom." And with that he turns and walks out the door, closing me in the darkness. Taking a deep breath, I allow my eyes to adjust.

"Is there anyone else here?" I breathe.

"Oi, is that you—unicorn?" the baritone of Xavier echoes from the ceiling.

"Angel? They've got you trussed up already? What did you do?" I blink, just making out the outline of his enormous wings against the skylight.

"The Queen tasked me to be her record keeper, to catalog her menagerie. And what better vantage point than here," he asks mockingly.

"I'm surprised she was up and about to see you," I scratch my head. "From all tales, she's fallen quite ill."

"Ah, she hasn't been here in person. Her words were relayed through her seer," Xavier calls.

I shiver. The royal seer is a blind Fae whose gift is mind magic. Her white orbs seem to dig into your very soul, they say. I've been lucky to avoid her thus far. I've got a feeling that my luck has just worn out.

"Hey, aren't you supposed to be in your other—?" Xavier cuts himself short,

"Yeah. I need a cover story, stat."

"I gotchu. Let me think on it for a few," Xavier states then falls quiet leaving me to my own thoughts. How the fuck did I get myself here?

Needing to keep moving, I use one big feather to sweep the others into a pile. It feels almost sacrilegious, but I plop down onto the softness with a sigh. I could shift and possibly break out of this cage, but I'd still be in the viewing room with no way out.

"Could you fake amnesia? Have they talked to you at all? Maybe say you woke up in the woods near wherever Altair found you," Xavier offers.

"Hmm. Yeah but who am I and how did I get here?"

"That's for them to find out. Hopefully, before that we can make our break," Xavier states. "Now shush and rest before the shitshow that tomorrow will bring."

He has a point. It won't do me any good to stay up and be delirious when they question me tomorrow, I need to be in top shape if I'm going to pull this off. Hoping our plan works, I snuggle into Flame's feathers and drift off.

※

I'm thrust to my feet, not a way that I would normally like to be awakened.

"Up with you, the King is ready to question you," Altair laughs.

Shit, I didn't even have time to think of a cover, I

guess faking a lost identity is the only way to go. Altair shoves me roughly in front of him, but doesn't tell me which direction to go, so I stop, Altair prods me to keep moving.

"This would be easier to navigate if you told me which way to go," I mutter.

"Are you talking to me?" Altair asks.

"I don't see anyone else here, do you?" I ask. I know that this isn't the best way to get out of my imprisonment but if I'm going to fake amnesia, I better start now.

"If we weren't headed to the King at this moment, I'd take you to the square and teach you some manners," Altair comments as he nudges me to the right.

I, of course, know the way to the room we are headed to but there isn't any way I can let him know that.

"Is that so?" I ask, knowing by now he probably wants to pummel me into the tile floor.

"Shut up, we are here. You will only speak to the King when you're asked a question. If you speak out of turn, there will be a punishment. Fun for me, pain for you," he says with an evil grin.

"Sounds like a party," I comment and this time, Altair doesn't hold back. He slams an elbow into my ribs. I sputter and cough but he makes me stand up before we step into the King's room.

"Altair, who is this guest?" the King asks, his gaze falling on me.

"This man was outside my charge's tower, he hasn't

given me a name or a reason why he would be there. I have never seen him before," my jailer tells the King.

"What do you have to say for yourself? Who are you and why are you in my kingdom?" the King asks as he looks down his nose at me.

Before I can reply, another of the guards steps forward and hits me with the hilt of his sword on my cheek. The impact is jarring and I spit out the blood that has formed in my mouth.

"How dare you make a mess of the King's Throne room," the guard that hit me states in disgust.

"This was your doing, I was about to answer the King and you hit me. What was I supposed to do with the blood?" I question the Fae.

"Swallow it," he sneers.

"First of all, eww. Secondly, maybe you shouldn't have hit me," I argue. All this does is earn me another blow, but this time to the ribs.

"Enough," the King says as he stands. "Fetch Zelle, I have a feeling this one will need her healing, he will not talk easily."

Altair does a weird little bow and races out of the room. I almost wish that I could just shift and show my other form, but it would be worse for me to do that now. Better to keep up this stupid act for now.

"I'll ask you once more, who are you and why are you here?" the King asks me.

"I do not know who I am or how I got here," I lie.

"Is that so? There is no way for you to simply just stumble onto my lands. So, either a spy or just a dumbass. Maybe both," the King muses.

He nods toward my attacker, "Gunter, you know what to do."

This Gunter fellow lands another blow to my ribs, causing me to double over in pain.

"I'm telling you, I don't know how I got here. I was stumbling through the trees when I came upon that tower. The first Fae I saw was that Altair lad and he took me as a prisoner. I haven't done anything wrong other than cross into your lands." I state, hoping they will believe my story.

But the punch to my jaw tells me that Gunter doesn't care one way or the other.

Blood drips onto the floor once more and he hits me again. "I told you, no spitting on the tile."

"If you would stop hitting me, I'll stop bleeding," I growl, aching to shift and give Gunter a mouthful of hoof.

"Looks like he doesn't want to talk, go get Cavill. Maybe a good lashing will loosen his tongue," the King smirks.

I'm not surprised. It's not like I haven't been in this position before. The King and Queen feed on bloodshed.

"Cavill will get you to tell us why you're truly here. The ones he can't get to talk, well, they don't talk afterward either," the King laughs.

Which can only mean that Cavill is a murderer. I gulp as a mountain of a Fae enters the hall. A tinge of fear runs down my spine at the unfamiliar guard. He is the most muscled Fae I've ever seen. How am I going to get out of this now?

"What do we have here?" Cavill asks the King.

"Someone that doesn't want to be truthful. I figure that you and your whip could get those lips moving," the King muses.

Before I know it, I am forced to my knees.

"Hands on the ground, do not move after I strike you. If you do, I will not hesitate to do it again," Cavill tells me before adding, "This is going to hurt me more than it hurts you."

I doubt that. The first lash hits me and I almost squeal. Taking a beating on my horse hide is much easier than this frail, human skin. Quivering with pain, I look up just as the throne room doors are thrown open. To my dismay, Altair reappears with Zelle following.

This isn't something I want her to see, but I have no way of stopping it.

As the leather makes contact on my skin again, a scream leaves Zelle's lips. The pain and heartache in her voice will surely haunt my nightmares. Try as I might, I can't keep my eyes off of her. Hoping no one sees, I mouth for her not to recognize me.

"Stop this!" Zelle rushes forward, hair flying in every direction. Her tiny frame stands between Cavill and myself as if she were ten times his size.

"Princess, move or I will hit you along with this trespasser," Cavill grits.

My heart stops when Zelle lassos her hair around his whip and jerks it from his hand. "I am no princess. And you will do no such thing," she steps on the whip and turns her attention to the King. "Why summon me during one of your dreadful punishments? I bear the pain of your anger enough when I have to wipe their blood away, now you wish me to witness it, too? What more will you put me though while you lock me away? Why do either this man or myself deserve your wrath on this day?"

The King's brows furrow and he studies Zelle for a long, quiet minute. Everything in me wants to shift and carry her away on my back. Flight mode has certainly been activated. Instead, I sweat bullets as I try to decipher the King's small movements as he straightens in his throne.

"I knew your royal blood would come forth if we pushed you enough," the King smirks as he settles back in the large cushion of his chair. "Know this, child, you are a princess, and that makes your slave price ever so much more valuable. Tell me, have you seen this man before?"

Zelle's jaw hangs open. I know for a fact she had no idea of her parentage, I'm as shocked as she is. Time seems to stand still as Zelle musters her voice.

"If I'm such a prize, why do you treat me so poorly? Surely, even you understand that better treatment is returned in the work you ask of us? I demand you to stop whipping this—trespasser as you call him."

It's not lost on me that Zelle avoided the King's question. She's not one to lie. *Stars, let us both get out of this alive.*

Zelle

The throne room is so silent, one could hear a pin drop. Not even the wind dares to whisper through the open windows at this moment. I know I shouldn't have stood up to the King, but I couldn't help myself. Too many things hit me all at once. Seeing Kain being lashed was enough to throw me over the edge, but the King dropping the information about me being a princess like it was no big deal was too much. Who am I?

After what feels like an eon, the King rises. Looking down his nose at me, he snaps for one of the servants. Some whispering ensues between him and the very wiry-looking fellow before Thayer returns his attention to me. As his golden eyes glitter, I truly see him for the first time.

Beneath the veneer, he is a broken old Fae. The stalwart frame and gleaming blond hair is all a mirage, a glamor he puts on. Underneath the magic, he is frail with white-clouded eyes. His time is nearing and whatever ails him is something beyond healing. Maybe it is not the Queen who is sick after all?

"For your insolence, I should lay you next to this vagabond and let Cavill have his way," Thayer paces the tiny stage holding his throne. "But, as a gesture of goodwill and honoring your heritage—I will cast you both to the dungeons until I can think more clearly. Guards," he waves his hand, "take them out of my sight."

Kain growls and I elbow him to be quiet as we're dragged from the room. There's no use in fighting, what's done is done. At least Kain won't be abused anymore this day. If we're lucky, Thayer will forget about us for a few days. Though his anger is hot, his memory is fleeting. At least from my limited experience.

I can barely move my feet fast enough to keep up with Altair, Gunter, and Cavill as we're ushered out of the palace. The sun seems to jump from behind a cloud, casting an accusatory beam right in my eye. Blinking, I turn my face to the side and notice Wren marching our way face reddened.

"What is going on?" He catches up to Altair, glaring at me.

"She stood up for this ruffian and now they are both to be sent to the dungeon," Altair states.

"Zelle," Wren grits out my name as if it hurts his tongue. "I can't believe you'd risk yourself for this stranger."

He grabs me from Altair. "I'll take her down."

"Suit yourself. I'd better go back and placate Thayer," Altair sighs before dropping out of the group.

Wren's grip is tight, but he isn't hurting me as he

usually would. I stare at the ground as we make our way to the far side of the kingdom. Everything has gone to hell. How are we going to escape from the dungeons? The tower, sure—but the dungeons are deep within Wolgast and heavily guarded.

"I've really fucked up." My lips tremble and I dare a glance at Kain. His head hangs low and a tear drops from his eye.

We cross through the royal gardens. The scent of lavender clings to my dress, almost mockingly as we enter the tunnels that lead down into the very bowels of Faerie. As soon as the gate shuts behind us, the world seems upside down. The only light comes from dark-red crystals growing in the walls.

The only good thing about being in this place is that my hair doesn't hold me down as it does topside. It's almost as if we are swimming, the way our clothes and hair sway around us. As my eyes adjust, I take note of every step we take in preparation for our escape.

"How far does the King mean to send them?" Wren asks Gunter and Cavill, who are dragging Kain between them.

"He didn't say," Cavill replies. "But he has a soft spot for the girl, so we best keep them whole. You know how fast things can turn down at the bottom," his tips his head.

"Aye, best not to take them there. The middle then? I'd rather not be in here all night," Wren complains.

Cavill nods, then takes a sharp right. The turn came so fast, it almost seemed as if he disappeared. Startled, I let out a squeak and trip on my skirt. Wren catches me with an arm around my middle.

"Careful," Wren whispers.

When he stands me back up, our noses touch and I freeze sucked in by his deep-purple eyes. Something about the way he looks in the red light catches me off guard. "Thank you." I manage to make my lips move enough to answer. Wren's lips turn up ever so slightly and my stomach flutters.

"Oi, you coming or what?" Gunter bellows from ahead and the moment is broken. Wren shakes his head, grabs me by the arm and marches me forward at a faster pace than before.

I don't know what would have happened if we had one more moment, but part of me wanted to find out. Wren is a mystery, a very striking one.

With as much time as I've spent with Wren, I've become all too familiar with every small detail from his long, silvery locks to his well-defined cheekbones. Not to mention the wrestler's shoulders that are part of his 'burly guard' physique which he maintains with hours of workouts each day. He moves like a tiger and his purple eyes twinkle when he is angry. He's been a thorn in my side, but delicious eye candy all the same.

"Finally," Gunter growls as we turn another bend. The hall widens and a door appears before us as if he wished it to do so. Gunter raises one hand, places it in some grooves in the wall and the door opens.

As we step over the threshold, a light flares to life, this time blue in hue. Every few feet down the corridor is a door with a small barred window at the top. I count six cells on each side before we stop. Cavill opens the door on our left and pushes Kain inside.

"Wait!" I cry out before he shuts the door. "At least let me heal him before you lock the cell."

"Not a chance," Gunter spits on the ground and slams the metal door, blocking Kain from my sight but for his eyes.

I slip out of Wren's hold and grab the bars of the window hoping for one last look before I'm taken. Cavill grabs me roughly away and slaps me in the face. He tangles a hand in my hair and yanks me to the floor, then steps over me with a smirk on his pointy face. I refuse to let him see me cry. This latest indignity may bend me, but it won't break me. I won't let it.

Cavill and Gunter split and walk around Wren, laughing as they leave. "We've got to check on the bottom floor, Put her in the last cell and see yourself out!" Cavill shouts over his shoulder.

I watch their backs until they disappear beyond the doorway and then I droop, catching my face with my hands. Wren carefully lifts me by my elbow and I follow him to the cell beside Kain without a word, thankful for his moment of gentleness.

"I don't understand you," Wren walks me into the cell. "How can you be so good, even after all that has been done to you?"

As if seeing Wren for the first time, I look up. There's emotion written in the wrinkles of his forehead that I've yet to see. "It is who I am," I shrug.

Wren sighs. "They feed the prisoners down here once a day. I'll come down to check on you tomorrow.

Maybe the King will have forgotten your slight and I can take you back home."

He turns to leave and my throat burns. "That tower is not my home!" My voice trembles at the end, so I close my mouth tight, gritting my teeth. Wren's shoulders drop, but he doesn't reply. He closes the cell door quietly before his footsteps recede down the hall. Not until I hear the other door shut do I stick my face to the small window.

"Can you hear me?" I whisper.

"Yeah, babe, I'm here. Call me Auris," Kain's voice seems to enter my cell and caress my face.

"What are we going to do now?" I hold back tears.

"You are going to listen very carefully," a familiar female voice calls from behind me. Startled, I pivot on one foot and almost fall when I see Prax lounging on the bed as if she were the Queen and I'd been called to service.

"What? How did you get here?" I stammer.

"This shell of mine may look weak, I can assure you I am anything but. Now why is it that you didn't come to me as I requested?" she questions, as she sits up a little more.

"I'm sorry to have failed you. We were about to come to you, but Kain was caught and tortured. Please understand that I want and need your help," I say as I fall to my knees ready to beg if I have to.

"Get up, you kneel for no one," she orders as she makes a 'get up' motion with her hands. "The King wasn't lying when he said that you are a princess. What he didn't tell you was that you aren't from the Fae Realm at all."

She pauses for dramatic effect as I rise back to my feet. She starts again and says with air quotes, "Your 'Mother' stole you for your hair, you belong in the Human Realm."

"Is that where you are from? Have you come to help get me back there?" I ask.

"I came to this realm in search of my successor, of all the places I've been, there was no one worthy of my gifts. That was until I came here and found you. Even after all you have endured, your heart is still pure, but you will have to harden it for what is to come. There will be things that have to be done in order to secure your exit, that may include murder. Can you stomach that?" she asks.

"Will I have to harm the innocent?" I question.

"No, the gifts I promise you will help you on your quest of freedom which is intertwined with my specialty—vengeance. First you must train with your men and hone your knowledge for fighting. When you speak, breathe, and love as one unit, I will reappear. Only then will you be ready to lead your band of men to their freedom as well," she says as her shape begins to shimmer and she disappears.

"Wait, don't go!" I beg, "I'm not sure what you mean."

Her gifts, freedom, fight, and my men? Do I have men? Kain? I think he counts as one but who else is she talking about? There are too many questions running through my mind. I want to scream in frustration, but what good would it do?

"Auris, are you still awake?" I ask through the grate of my door.

"I am," he states.

"Can you teach me to fight?" I question.

"Why would you want to learn such a thing?" he asks in return.

"It's a long story. Let's talk more tomorrow, you need your rest, that will be the only way for you to heal," I whisper before plopping onto the cot the Goddess left empty.

"As you wish, Princess," he mutters.

I toss and turn on the slight mattress. I'm not tired but what else is there to do in my darkened cell? I sigh as I take in the state of my hair. That asshole, Cavill did a number on it when he put his hands in it. I long for the brush from my tower and at that thought, I think of Pascal. Will he think that I abandoned him? I do my best to think of anything else, so I do what I can, running my fingers through my locks. I hum a little tune as I work and my hair starts to glow, lighting up my cell.

I have always been afraid of the dark, well not the dark but what could be waiting in there for me. It's a relief to see every inch of the small cell lit up. Even better, to my utter surprise a familiar green blur races in under the door.

"Oh Pascal, you have come for me!"

"Of course, you are my friend. The only one in this place that showed kindness. I may be a chameleon but I have feelings. So, when Wren came back muttering under his breath about you being a stupid girl for getting yourself locked up, I came as fast as my little legs would carry me," he says as he moves along my hair, helping me to untangle the knots.

"Well, I thank you. You being here makes this place suck a little less," I say as I start to hum once more.

With the two of us, it doesn't take as long to get my hair back in its braided form.

"Thank you, Pascal, you were just who I needed right now," I tell him with a little pet on his head. "I promise to take you with me when I get out of this hellhole."

"Do you have a plan?" he questions as he moves into my lap.

"I've got the start of one. What do you know about fighting?"

"Not much, but Wren does a lot of practice drills. Maybe you can ask him?" Pascal offers up.

I laugh a little, "This land would have to freeze over before Wren would give me the time of day, let alone training lessons." I say, but my mind keeps drifting over the tenderness he showed me today.

"That's too bad, but I do like the cold. It never really bothers me, anyway," he says as he smiles up at me.

"Then I guess before we sleep, we better pray for icy weather," I giggle as I recline into the bed, trying to find a comfy spot to rest.

"How is it that after all that's been done to you, you still have faith in a higher power? Something that will get you out of here and on to a better life?" my little friend queries.

"If I don't, the only thing left is to give up. The only way I would do that is if I die and I have no plans for doing that for many years to come. The King just informed me of my royal blood and the Goddess said I'm of the Human Realm. If I can learn to fight, I will escape this place and return to where I truly belong. Only then will I know what home is," I sigh.

Zelle

The next thing I know, I'm woken up by a commotion outside my door. Curious, I rise and cross the room. Peeking through the grate, I gasp when a feather brushes my cheek. Xavier is herded into the cell next to me—which is a surprise in itself, but Flynn is tossed in with him.

That answers who Prax has determined are my men.

Moving out of sight, I lean on the wall beside the door. How is our being in the dungeon together helpful? My head spins with more questions. Before I can even blink, the door to my cell opens.

"Here's your breakfast," an unfamiliar Fae sets a tray by the door and leaves, sliding the heavy metal lock into place loudly.

Part of me wants to give up and lay in my bed, but the other is determined to figure out how to fight. Sitting against the door, I scoop the porridge into my mouth and think of fresh bread. Pascal joins me, and I urge him to dip his face into the food.

"Zelle?" Kain's voice is barely loud enough for me to

hear. Setting my plate down, I stand up to the small window in the door. "Yes?"

"Stay away from the joining wall."

"Okay," I answer, curious.

With nothing left to do but wait, I slide back down and resume eating. The porridge is lumpy but edible. Pascal clenches my shoulder as he watches the wall with me. I'm surprised when he runs down my arm and slides under the door, but I shrug it off. He's probably going out to catch bugs.

A few minutes later, Kain's horn bursts through the wall. Excited, I put the tray down and stand. One by one, he bores four holes in the shape of a diamond by the corner of the wall. I want to go over and look through them, but I don't dare as I need to figure out what's next.

"Zelle," Kain whispers through one of the holes, and I race over.

"Hey," I laugh, unable to contain the joy of seeing even a tiny part of his face.

"Where is your cot?" Kain seems rushed.

"It's against the other wall," I answer.

"Okay, good. I'm going to drill a few more holes to make it easier for me to kick out this portion of this wall. If anyone comes, put your cot in front of the space, okay?"

"Got it!" I answer.

Kain is good as his word. After a few more holes, I hear his hooves connecting with the wall. Slowly, a spot opens just big enough for one of us to crawl through. Before he can shift, I slide into his cell and wrap my arms around his neck. His fur is damp with sweat from the exertion, but he nuzzles against me. In that moment of connection, I realize he is mine. I've never had a feeling like this one. Ever.

"Kain, I'm so glad to see you," I sigh as I wrap my hair around his neck. It's nothing for me to give back, healing him of the pain from working so hard.

Amid my glowing hair, Kain shimmers and shifts into his human form, enveloping me in his strong arms before I can argue about modesty. Hugging his unicorn form was comforting, but this form made me warm all over.

"Zelle," Kain tips my mouth upward and brushes his plush lips against mine. Eyes wide open in surprise, my nose bumps into him before I rise on my toes, fully accepting his offering. Kain cradles my head with one hand and wraps the other around my back, holding me as if I were fragile. Wrapping my arms around his neck, I lean into him and lose myself in the slow rhythm of his tongue dipping in and out of my mouth. My hair glows bright, and then the light fades as Kain is fully healed.

"I have so much to tell you," I whisper, breaking the kiss.

Kain smiles down at me, his blond hair cascading around us like a curtain. "Can it wait? Let's enjoy our stolen moment, for who knows how long it will last."

With one swoop of his arms, he carries me over to his cot and lays beside me. His hands explore as we fall back into kissing. Everything in me sets aflame. Tracing the valley of his spine, I urge Kain to move over me. His body covers mine in the most intimate embrace, and I sigh with pleasure wishing my skirt wasn't acting as a barrier. I want his skin on mine. I haul it up with one hand, freeing my legs to wrap around him. Kain groans, leaning up on his elbows.

"Zelle, if we don't stop now, I won't be able to control myself," he says between dropping kisses on my neck.

"Then don't stop," I urge, rolling my hips against his. I've never been with a man, but my body seems to know what it wants.

"Have you ever?" He props his head on his hand, tracing my lips with a finger.

I shake my head, my face flushing with embarrassment. Kain's face softens, and he brushes his lips over mine, light as a feather. "Maybe we should wait then? This isn't the most romantic of surroundings, Zelle. You deserve more."

"If I'm right about what the next weeks hold for us, things will likely worsen. I don't care about where we are; I care that I'm with you," I place my palm on his beating heart.

Kain's lids lower, and a heat flashes in his eyes that wasn't there before. He shimmers all over, just as he does before a shift. I take a breath, staring at the angles of his jaw, memorizing this moment in time so that I'll have something to hold on to if it all falls apart. Ever so gently, Kain raises my dress over my head, leaving me bare naked in the cool room. My nipples pebble, and my stomach churns in anticipation.

"Then, let me worship you," Kain's voice is smooth

as velvet as he crawls over me again. I open my arms, expecting him to come in for more kissing but instead, he dips his head between my thighs. An explosion of sensation washes over me.

"Oh," I squeak, tensing as his tongue wanders my nether parts.

"Relax, love," Kain massages my thighs, kissing his way up to my knees. "I want you to be completely ready before I take you."

I'm ready now, I think, but the small fires Kain lights along my skin tell me differently. Deciding to catalog this in my memory bank, I lay my head back and close my eyes. Kain's tenderness as he touches and kisses each part of my body warms my heart and loosens the nerves that tied knots in my belly. By the time his face hovers over mine again, I'm a gooey mess of a human.

"Hey there," Kain grins as he brushes a strand of hair away from my face.

"Hi," I answer languidly.

"Zelle, I want you to touch me," Kain takes my hand and guides it down between his legs. I gasp when my fingers slide along his shaft. It's hard and soft all at once, so different than I'd expected. Taking my time, I wrap my fingers around his dick and squeeze a little, testing it out. Kain covers my mouth with a kiss and traces a line down my navel until his finger dips into my wetness. I know physically what happens next, but my mind is exploding with the small circular movements of his digit.

"Please," I break away, bucking against his hand.

"Zelle, I love you," Kain sighs, gripping my jaw like

we're in the middle of a long goodbye instead of this heated moment.

"I love you," I whisper, gripping his shaft tighter. Hoping against hope that we both make it out of this place.

He groans and grabs my hand, placing it above my head. My heart races as I watch him center himself and thrust his hips forward. I'd expected pain, but I didn't expect a mixture of pleasure to follow. Kain inches his way into my core until our bodies are as close as two can be.

Our eyes meet, and I lift my head for another kiss. His tongue dives into my mouth, and his hips begin moving slowly. The pain eases, and in its place is divine ecstasy. Grabbing onto his back with my free hand, I lift my hips in rhythm. Before I know it, the muscles in my core tighten, and waves of pleasure begin to ripple over me. Throwing my head back, I let out a small moan. Kain dips his head, kissing my neck as he plunges ever deeper. His hands tighten over mine, and his lips form an o. He pulls out of me all at once, holding his member and spending his seed into the cover. I cuddle his side, wiping the sweaty strands of hair from his face.

Kain pulls me into an embrace and curls his body around mine. We lay quietly as our breathing slows. My heart soaring, I trace lines along his muscular arm.

"Was it very painful?" he whispers in my ear.

"No, it was perfect," I answer with a smile. "We still need to talk. I met a Goddess last night," I turn toward him.

"Oh, how's that?" he asks.

"She was right there, in my cell. Her name is Prax and she's dying. She told me that before she passes, she wants to give her powers to another," I recount, not really believing the story now that I'm hearing it out loud.

"Is that so? And are you who she wishes to pass them to?" he guesses.

"Yes, but I have to learn to fight before she will come back. Can you teach me?" I ask, looking up at him.

"I am good in a tussle but I'm no warrior," he admits. "If I'm in a fight, I'm usually in my other form."

"Well, maybe one of the others? Wren brought Xavier and Flynn down earlier. Prax said she would bring my men down here, whatever that means." I flush, feeling uncomfortable.

"Do you trust them?" Kain whispers.

"I have to. I believe the Goddess does, so that's good enough for me. If they are what we need to get out of here, so it shall be," I state matter of factly.

When I look up, Kain's forehead is creased with worry.

"Don't fret, you are still my best unicorn," I smirk at him.

The compliment does the trick as his smile returns. "Okay then. Maybe I should cross over to your room and knock out the wall that separates them," Kain offers.

"So, you believe me? I mean about the Goddess?" I stare into his eyes, trying to detect a lie.

"Zelle, you risked your life and comfort for me, why wouldn't I?" he asks with a faint look of hurt.

"Maybe because it sounds crazy." I shrug.

"I'm a unicorn shifter in the land of the Fae. I live crazy," Kain says as he leans in for another kiss.

"Oi, are you going to start knocking the wall down? Or do we have to just listen to the two of you fuck again?" Flynn's voice fills the hallway. Thank the stars no one else is being held in this block.

My cheeks flush, but Kain is the one to speak up. "You talk to my girl like that again and I'll make you watch," he remarks.

"Jokes on you, I think I'd be into that," Flynn counters.

Kain turns to me, rolling his eyes as he says, "That one's a keeper for sure."

A laugh escapes my lips and even with us being in a dungeon, I've never felt more free. Taking Kain by the hand, I leave the small cot. Rummaging around, I pull on my dress. Kain doesn't bother with clothing, he slips through the hole in the wall naked as a jaybird. I can't say I mind at all, the view is —something.

Following Kain into my room, I stand near the door. Kain moves my bed over to cover the first hole, then cracks his knuckles. He winks at me, before shouting, "Xavier, can you close your wings for me buddy? I know that Zelle can heal you but if she's gonna train she'll need her strength."

"Maybe you should have thought of that before you had your way with her, huh?" Flynn asks.

"I have half a mind to leave him over there, but how would that be fair to Xavier?" Kain asks me.

"Not fair at all, I think that Flynn is just one that likes to hear the sound of his own voice. Something we will have to get used to," I shrug.

"Okay you two stay close to the door, I'll try and contain the explosion, but these walls are unpredictable." Kain calls out.

"We are ready when you are," Flynn answers.

Kain shimmers into his other form and starts to work on the barrier that separates us from the others. As the holes appear, I take note of Flynn's waving from the other side, a smile wide on his face.

"So we meet again," he states.

I roll my eyes and wait for Kain to finish up the demolition. Anxious to check Xavier over, I bite at my nails. I don't want to imagine the tortures the King has put him through. Flynn, on the other hand, is going to be fine with that silver tongue of his.

"Took your sweet ass time," Flynn states as he walks over the rubble.

Kain shifts back to his human form, grabs my blanket and wraps it around his waist, and takes a seat on my cot without so much as a glance toward Flynn.

I cross the room, heading to Xavier and start to check him over, "Have they been beating you again?"

"Not since I saw you last, but big mouth got me thrown down here, he told them we were friends," Xavier growls.

"What? I want details?" I demand, walking around him. I know that he said he was fine, but I've been here long enough to know how the guards toy with the prisoners.

"He wouldn't shut up," he sighs.

Flynn circles around us, before whispering in my ear, "Did you miss me, baby?"

He places a hand on my shoulder and I shrug it off. Even if we are bound by the Goddess, he is a little too forward for me.

"Are you going to flirt with me or teach me to fight?" I ask, moving back toward Kain.

"Am I teaching the pony, too?" he asks, raising an eyebrow.

"Unicorn," Kain grits out.

"Start with me," I say, "Prax said I was the one that needed to learn. If Kain learns, that's a plus."

Flynn smirks, "Okay, are you ready for your first lesson?"

"I mean I don't have anywhere else to be," I joke.

"Funny, girl. I like that. If you'll join me in the middle of the cell," he starts, holding out a hand to me.

I take it and he pulls me close to him, he winks and moves to face me.

"Okay, I'm going to first show you some punches followed by some kicks. I want you to mimic my movements. Once you have them down, we will do some full contact," Flynn says.

"Full contact? As in hitting one of you three? Oh I don't know if I can do that," I tell him honestly.

"If you want to leave this place, you're gonna have to toughen up, do what it takes to escape," Flynn reminds me.

"I know you're right, it's just the healer in me that cringes away from the thought of harming another," I say honestly. "But make no mistake, I will do whatever it takes to free all four of us from this hell."

Flynn's smile returns, "There's the spirit I knew was hidden in there. Okay, now let's get to work.

Zelle

I don't know how long Flynn made me punch and kick the air, but one thing is for certain I've got to get pants. Fighting in a dress sucks ass. Sweat dripping down my neck, I flop down on the cot.

"I need a break," I heave.

"Here, drink up," Kain hands me a canteen and I take three long gulps greedily.

"You do realize they're going to be bringing food soon?" Pascal skitters under the door. The three guys all stare at the chameleon before turning their heads to me.

"What? As if you haven't seen a talking animal before?" I scoff, crossing the room and offering a finger for Pascal to climb. "Sounds like you three need to go back to your cells and hide the damage as much as possible. Shouldn't be too hard since it's ridiculously dark down here. Just bring your Fae lights near the door."

There's a murmur between the guys, then they stand. Flynn is the first through the wall, blowing a kiss as he exits. Xavier comes over and gives me a light hug before disappearing, leaving Kain standing in the middle of the room with my blanket still around his waist.

"I'll be back as soon as the coast is clear," he pulls me in for a kiss. My body trembles, remembering our tryst and I sigh. All the more reason to get out of this place.

Kain leaves me standing with my blanket as he struts across the room naked. Enjoying the view, I grin. To avoid this in the future, it would probably be best to ask Wren for my old robe. Not that I hate the sight of Kain's tight ass, but keeping it covered is less distracting.

"I can smell food. Hurry and move the cot," Pascal nudges me with his snout.

Thankfully, Kain is smart. The hole is easily hidden by placing the cot against the wall and hanging the blanket off the side. Satisfied, I move my Fae light to the front corner, near the door before sitting on the bed to wait. Who knows if the guard will be one of mine or not.

The jangle of keys is the first indication that someone has arrived. Footsteps stop outside of Kain's door first. "Time to eat," Altair's familiar voice calls.

"Zelle," Wren opens my door, "here's your food."

I rise and cross the room so that he can hand the tray to me. Before I can step back, he clears his throat. Curious as to what else he wants, I lock eyes with him.

"I also brought a few things from your room. King Thayer won't tell us how long he intends you to be here," Wren purses his lips as he sets a bag beside the wall. "I'd advise you not to start any more trouble but there's hardly a way for you to do that here." Wren opens his mouth to say more, but Altair darkens the door with a raised eyebrow.

"When you're done, slide the tray under the door. The night slaves will pick it up," Wren's tone is back to his usual harshness.

Confused as ever at his hot and cold temperament, I nod and turn toward my bed. The door closes and I sit down to eat. I can't help but smile when I realize there's fresh bread on my tray as well as a few slices of ham. I don't know what's gotten into Wren, but I'm not going to question better food after all the exertion.

Before I realize it, I've gobbled the entire tray. With a full belly, I could almost lay down and sleep except for the fact that I know we need to start planning our escape. Shoving my tray under the door, I cross the room and uncover the hole leading to Kain.

"Psst," I whisper. "You ready?"

"If he isn't, we are," Flynn smiles as he enters through the other hole.

Honestly, I don't know how I didn't think to try and cover that one, too. Not that I have anything to do so with, but still. I'm lucky Wren wasn't looking very hard when he came in. Resigned to suffer through more of Flynn's flirting, I wave him and Xavier inside. Kain takes a minute before appearing as well.

"How will we tell time in this dungeon?" I think out loud. Exhaustion is nearing, I can feel it. Learning fighting moves after my first sexual experience probably wasn't the brightest idea.

"I can tell when the sun rises," Xavier replies. "It's one of the weird angel traits that I can't honestly explain as it serves no real purpose."

"Okay. Any other special abilities you have? Particularly ones that would help us get out of here?" I pace the room, eyeing my emerging army.

"Well," Xavier sighs. "When I'm not in Faerie, I have super speed and strength, I can summon angel cry to demolish things, teleport, and rewrite memories. All of my powers are dampened here, though. We aren't in the realm of the Almighty, afterall. I can still fly and I have some of my strength, but nothing else really." A pained expression crosses Xavier's face.

"It's more than most," I take his hand in mine. "I need you."

Xavier's hazel eyes turn golden as they bore into mine. He tightens his grip and we stand there frozen. A soft tingling starts at my palm and the hairs rise on my arms. Giving into the moment, I close the distance and bury my face in the crook of his neck. "I need an army. Be my soldier?" I plead.

Xavier kneels, one arm over his chest. "I'm yours for whatever may come. There's something about you that draws me in. Zelle, you are a true soul." He dips his head and closes his eyes as if in prayer.

"Yeah, I'm in, too, doll," Flynn cracks his knuckles. "No need to beg. I know my skills as a thief will come in handy."

"Now that that's settled," Kain shakes his head. "How do we get this Goddess to reappear?"

"That's just it, we don't," I step away from the group.

"She said I have to learn to fight and there's something about the way she said everything that..." I stop, unsure how to wrap my mind around the implication that I picked up from Prax. What if I'm wrong and she doesn't mean for them to be...to be what? I am losing my mind.

"She said we need to speak, breathe, and love as one unit," I finally blurt out. "I don't know what that means, but—"

Flynn interrupts me with a whistle."Seems pretty clear to me," Flynn whistles. "Looks like you got yourself a harem of men, blondie."

"A harem, huh? I have heard of men having those but not a woman," I note.

Flynn's smile widens, "How about a reverse harem? Since we've got a woman with three men."

"I like that," I smile, "So, does that mean I'm in charge?"

"As if there was any doubt of that," Kain pipes in.

His comment makes me laugh, and it's been a while since I have. It feels good to live in the moment and have a minute of joy. I almost feel whole, but there's something telling me that I have one more man to add to this harem. What I don't have is an inkling of who that would be. With the three here, I had a definite draw. Even Flynn, I think mostly because of his slick tongue, but it was there. I'm tired of being patient, I've been in a cage long enough, but there's nothing to do but wait for Prax.

"So, now that we've had some calories, are you

ready to continue your training?" Flynn asks, rubbing his hands together menacingly.

Xavier stands and extends a hand towards me, "I have made you a weapon. It may not be much, but it will help you with the weight of the real thing."

"Thank you, Xavier. How did you make this?" I question, holding it up for the other two to see.

"There are times that I molt and shed feathers. I knew that you wanted to train, so fighting with something in your hand can be what you need to get the advantage," he says before stepping back.

"Thank you, Xavier. That is so kind of you. What kind of weapon would this mimic?" I ask as I look it over.

"It would be like a dagger, a small but mighty blade for stabbing and slicing. Close contact only," the fallen angel tells me.

"Flynn, are you planning on close contact instruction in my training?" I ask as I raise a brow at him.

"I am now, as long as you don't stab me with that homemade shank," Flynn states.

"At this point in time, that's not a promise I can make." I wink before turning my attention to my quiet unicorn. "Kain, are you well?"

"I am, Princess. I'm just soaking all of this in, just as you, I have a lot to learn," he replies with a smile.

"Maybe you'd like to have some one-on-one time with Flynn? I can train with Xavier and my weapon," I offer up.

"That's a great idea," Flynn pipes in. "We can return

to your cell or go to mine, that will give us some room to stretch out."

"I'll follow you," Kain states with a wave like lead the way.

I watch as they head into Flynn's cell, realizing that it's just Xavier and I here now.

"Are you ready to start? You can wield your weapon and practice your punches and kicks on me," the Fallen Angel suggests.

"What if I hurt you?" I question, not sure this is the best course of action.

"Are you not the Princess that has magical hair? I don't think that you will be able to really harm me, but on the off chance that happens, I have the best healer standing in front of me right now," he smiles.

"You think too highly of me," I blush.

"I speak the truth," he tries to assure me.

"Well, I guess we should get to work," I sigh, not really into all this fighting but I know it's something I need to do.

"First of all, you aren't holding it correctly," he says, walking behind me and moving my arm into the right position. "Think of this being an extension of your body, you are to use it as you would your arm."

With his hand over mine, he guides me to fluid movements. Once we have done it a few times, he releases me and returns to standing in front of me.

"Now, attack me," he states.

"Can't we just run some more drills first? I really don't want to injure you," I tell him.

He sighs and shakes his head no. "You have to hit me with it to hurt me."

Oh, so he's mister confident now? We will see about that. I take a step toward him, trying to strike him with the small blade.

We go through this little dance and I have yet to mark him.

"Why is hitting you so hard?" I complain.

"I could let you, but for what is to come you will need to know that it's not a simple task," Xavier replies.

"I never wanted any of this, just freedom. My fake mother stole me and then used me to pay off her debts. I didn't even know that I was a princess until they were beating Kain," I tell him.

"Freedom is one thing I have yet to taste. God was my master, until I rejected that and was sent to Earth. I'm not too sure how I ended up here," he says.

"I've heard rumors that the Fae leave this realm and travel to others just to steal workers. So, that's probably what happened to you," I guess.

"Well, that is something we need to end, but let's focus on getting out of here first," Xavier states.

A cry of pain comes from the darkened cell next to mine. My heart rate races as Xavier and I race over to find Flynn holding his nose.

"What happened?" I ask Kain.

"We were just practicing punches and his face got in my way. I didn't mean to hurt him," he tells us.

"I figured one of us would get hurt, just not Flynn here as he is the teacher," I remark as I bend down toward him. "Can you move your hands away and let me have a look?"

He huffs and does as I ask, there is some blood trickling down his face and his nose isn't the same shape it was when he and Kain started sparing.

"It's not that bad," I say, pulling my braid over my shoulder. "I'll have you fixed up in no time."

Since it's just a small injury, I don't unbraid my hair, just set it on his face and start my little tune.

There's a little pop and I know it's his nose righting itself, so I step back and admire his once again handsome face.

"Thank you," he mutters as he stands and wiggles his nose. "Maybe that's enough training for the day."

T he four of us retreat into the darkest corner of my cell, that way if any of the guards come they won't be able to see us. Not that we've seen many guards since we were brought down, but still. There's always Wren who seems to have made it his job to check in on me from time to time..

"So, Flynn," I start, sitting cross legged on the cool floor, "how's it you came to be here?"

"Well, I was tasked to steal something for a queen and when I did the job but didn't return with the goods, she sent an army of men to bring me in," he states.

It's hard to tell if he wears a smile or not, but from his tone, I believe he is.

"Why didn't you just hand it over to her?" I ask.

"Well, you see, I sold it off to the highest bidder," he replies.

"Why would you do that? You didn't think she would have your head?" Kain asks.

I think he shrugs his shoulders, "Most of the time, when I double-cross someone, they send one or two men for me. I am handy with a blade, so I normally don't have a problem with taking care of them myself. But this queen meant business, it took all the guards to subdue me," he answers.

"That explains all the men we saw with you, when they brought you in," I say, placing a hand on Kain's.

"Yes, we both thought it was odd for so many guards on one prisoner. I guess we know why now," Kain adds.

"You realize getting out of here is a long shot, right?" Xavier leans against the wall, his arms folded. "This isn't any prison. We are in Faerie."

The room goes quiet as we all soak in Xavier's words. Of course, I know it's a long shot, but I'm afraid if I voice my doubts, I'll give them power. Everything has meaning. Words spoken in Faerie have a way of twisting their way into being. Crossing the space between us, I gently lay a finger on Xavier's lips. "Down here words have more power than anywhere else, be careful what you say," I whisper.

Xavier's eyes spark with the same golden glow I saw before and he grabs my wrist. A squeak is all I manage before he pulls my body against his own. Our noses touch and his gaze bores into me like a hot knife.

"Then let me say again, I'm yours," Xavier vows before cupping my jaw and bringing his lips to mine.

Xavier's wings spring up, enclosing us in a feathered sanctuary. The small privacy is all I need to let down my guard. Leaning my head back, I lose myself in the feeling of his soft lips against mine. My knees weaken, so I wrap my arms around Xavier's neck as if I were drowning. There's a rightness that fills my soul as Xavier holds me close.

As quick as it happened, the kiss is over. Xavier touches his forehead to mine and gives me a wink before folding his wings behind his back again. Standing there with wobbly legs, I almost faint. There's something about knowing I kissed an angel that has me spinning.

Not to be outdone, Kain steps behind me and whispers in my ear, "I was yours first, don't forget."

"Oi, is this a race, mates? I don't mind being the last to the finish," Flynn laughs. "I'm yours, too, Blondie. You can save my smooch for a private affair." He ends with a smirk.

My thoughts whirl in and out of existence before I can pin them down. Looking over the three men in my prison cell, I'm a bit overwhelmed. There's never been anyone in my life who has wanted me for more than my hair. I want to question them and their loyalty, but the feeling in my chest is enough to put me at ease. I hadn't realized how long I stood there staring until Kain's voice filled the space.

"Look what you've all done," Kain leads me to the cot. "She's as frightened as a new foal."

Sitting down allows my mind to recuperate. "You know, usually a girl gets a guy, not three," I wrinkle my nose in mock disdain. "Is this really what we're doing? I would still take you all with me, even if—"

"Oi, none of that, Blondie. The boys and I have talked it through, we know what we're signing up for.

You are worth it," Flynn takes my hand and kisses it gently.

The sudden softness from the snarky one of the group tells me all I need to know. Nothing is ever predictable when in Faerie. If I also consider the fact that a Goddess has brought us together, the unusual relationship makes sense.

"A guard is coming," Pascal warns, skittering under the door, closing the conversation for good.

Acting fast, the guys slip through the walls into their own cells. Familiar footsteps near the door and I step toward the small window, curious. It's not time for them to feed us, so why is Wren down here?

"Zelle," Wren's voice sounds pained."The Queen has summoned you."

Not knowing what might happen next, I grab my mouth to hold the scream that tries to break free. "Why?" I manage to ask between my fingers.

"That, I do not know," Wren opens the door. His eye seems to drift toward the hole in the wall, but he says nothing.

Heart racing, I step out of the cell. Kain's eyes meet mine from behind his bars and I take a deep breath. "Will I be sent back here?"

"Zelle, stop asking me questions." Wren slams my cell door and takes me by the arm.

Taking one last look at Kain, I pinch my lips with worry. The unicorn's hazel eyes track me as Wren marches me away. Wren and I pass through the cell block door and into the red-tint of the main dungeon hall before he slows his pace.

"You risk too much fraternizing in the cells, Zelle," Wren stops me in a dark corner.

I almost defend myself, but determine it's best to keep my mouth shut. Instead, I tighten my lips and stare into his purple eyes. The anger I normally get from Wren is washed away somehow, which is confusing.

"Why do you care?" I whisper.

He purses his lips, turning his head away for a moment. "I don't want to," he grumbles before grabbing me by the arm and continuing out of the dungeon. I follow, dazed with his nonanswer. At least he hasn't hit me.

The last door is opened and we step out into the bright light of the morning. My eyes protest and I stumble, falling into Wren. Instead of him dragging me forward, he catches me in his arms. Our noses almost touch as he cradles me. With wide eyes, Wren quickly sets me on my feet and looks around as if he were in trouble. I'm not an idiot, there's something between us that wasn't there before. For an Elf to show affection to a slave, he would be risking everything.

"Wren?" I start to question, but the look he gives me shuts down any conversation.

"Walk. No talking."

He doesn't touch me again as we head toward the palace and I find myself aching for his hand on my arm. Inwardly kicking myself, I question my own sanity. As if a unicorn, angel, and human weren't enough to contend with, now I'm hung up on my jailor? What in the stars is happening to me?

"Took you long enough," Altair greets Wren from the palace entrance.

"She's clumsy." Wren grabs my arm again.

"Well, that is true. She's also a mess. You can't bring her to heal the Queen smelling like a latrine," Altair raises an eyebrow at him.

Wren scowls. "What am I supposed to do about that? The Queen doesn't like waiting."

"I'll take care of the Queen. You take her back to the tower and clean her up. Be fast." Altair opens the door and disappears before Wren can answer. The look on his face is of mild shock. I almost laugh, but then think better of it.

"Come then," he finally manages before pushing me toward the old tower.

I never thought I would despise the tower, but my time in the dungeon with those three men made me realize that they were my home.

"Why does the Queen want to see me now? After all this time?" I question Wren.

"You'll have to take that up with her," he says, not looking at me.

I stumble and grab his arm to brace myself from falling. He doesn't shake me off at first like he would if Altair were here and that confuses me, but I'm grateful that he stops me from falling on my face.

Once I have my footing, I release him before he grips my arm to move me faster. "We have to hurry, why are you slowing down?" Wren asks.

"I have no wish to meet the Queen. She has a thing for beheading people and I like mine right where it is," I state flatly as I sneak a peek at him. There's a faint smile on his lips.

It takes a moment for him to compose himself before he speaks again, "If you are called, you go, there is no other option. Count yourself lucky that Altair is allowing you a bath before she sees you."

He opens the little door at the bottom of my former home and the staircase is there to greet me. I do prefer them over that damn bucket, the bane of my existence.

Taking them two at a time, it's not long before I hit the landing and I don't wait for Wren as I strip and head straight to the bath. I can hear the steady flow as I enter the bathroom. Almost absently I use one finger to test the temperature but, of course, it's perfect. I let out a sigh as I step in.

"Best hurry," Wren states from behind me, causing me to jump.

As if in slow motion I start to fall backwards when Wren leaps forward and catches me.

"You need to be more careful, Princess," he mutters.

"What are you doing here?" I question, instead of thanking him.

"We don't have time to dawdle," he states as he releases his hold on me and I sink into the glorious water.

"I know, but that doesn't give you the right to watch me bathe. I am capable of doing so in a timely manner," I state, turning my back to him.

"There is no way that you can wash all that hair in the time limit we have," he scoffs.

"Oh and you're just the man to help me with that?" I ask, forgetting Wren is here to keep me in line."

"You dare to speak to me in that tone?" he questions.

"What are you going to do about it?" I snark back and instantly regret it. Thankfully, Wren just shakes his head.

"I don't have time for your games, Zelle." He sighs as he lathers his hands and begins rubbing the ends of my hair.

Not one to look a gift horse in the mouth, I hurry to wash my body while he continues with my hair. Wren begins to whistle a little as he works section after section of my long locks. Once I'm done with the essentials, I work a lather into my scalp.

"I got it from here," I tell him and he removes his hands from my hair but doesn't move away from the tub.

I raise an eyebrow. "I can't leave you, besides I have to dry your locks. We can't take you to the Queen, a wet mess," Wren answers.

I nod at him before submerging myself under the waterfall. I relish in the fact that I am truly clean even if I must see the Queen. I've missed this space.

All done, I rise from the liquid and exit the bath to stand in front of Wren, naked as a newborn babe. It's not as if modesty matters at this point. I am, however, unprepared for him to will his air magic around me. It's almost like standing in a warm, summer breeze. Eyes wide, I stare at Wren in wonder. He doesn't shy away from me, just concentrates on drying my body before my hair.

"I will have to warm the air and use more force for your hair. If it becomes too much let me know," Wren says kindly.

His new mannerisms strike me oddly, most of the time he is cold and distant as Altair, but lately, there have been rare moments like now that he is a whole new Fae.

"There, it should be dry," Wren states, stepping back from me, "Hurry and get on some clean clothes, or it will be both our heads."

I nod and rush to the trunk of clothes, rummaging for something that will be presentable to be in the Queen's presence. Settling on a silky pink-and-purple gown with white trim, I nod at my own choice. Since I've never met the Queen, I don't know what would please her or if she can be pleased at all.

Pulling it on in a rush, I do what I can with my hair as Wren motions for me to head back toward the stairs.

"We have to go, we've wasted too much time washing all that hair of yours," he says as we start our descent.

"I take it she's not very understanding?" I question, but don't stop.

"Well, I'd say she is very one way, as in her way or no way," he tells me.

"Of course," I comment but don't say anything more.

We step into the sunlight and continue back toward the castle.

"It's really beautiful here, too bad there are so many ugly people," I mutter to myself, not thinking Wren would reply.

"It hasn't always been this way, before the king took a bride there was a splendor to this place," Wren tells me.

"One woman did all this?" I ask, hoping he'll tell me more.

He gives me a solemn nod, "Fae children are rare and the one job of the Queen is to produce an heir. That has yet to happen."

So, he's telling me that all this death and imprisonment is simply because she can't have a child. Maybe I've been living my life all wrong, too complacent, maybe it's my turn to burn this world and take what's mine.

Before I can gather any more thoughts of rebellion, we step into the throne room and I lose any trace of my sense of self. The Queen is breathtaking. Her voluptuous frame is highlighted by her long, blue locks that seem to flow around her like a river. When our gazes meet, I'm frozen in place. Startling red eyes look me over as if I am an insect.

"So, this is the human my husband fusses over?" She leans forward, bracing her weight on her hands which causes no less than four footmen to step forward. "Leave me," she shoos them away with the flick of her wrist.

By looking at her, I would say she's the picture of health but I'm no doctor. Wren nudges me and I remember my manners, bowing low into a curtsy.

"She is the healer," Wren gestures to my hair.

There's a small tapping on the floor as the Queen crosses the space. A shiver of fear runs down my spine. It's too quiet in this large room filled with servants. No one even dares to breathe. My nerves build, but I keep my eyes downcast in hopes to remain unscathed.

"Well, what now? Do I cut her lovely hair off and eat it?" The Queen laughs, the sound so chilling goosebumps break out over my arms.

"Usually, she wraps the hair over the injured—" Altair offers but is quickly cut off by the beautiful tyrant.

"Ah yes, of course," The Queen steps up to me, her foot touching my skirts. "Then shall I stuff your beautiful hair into my womanly parts? Is that how we shall proceed?" Again with the laugh. Her voice bounces off the domed ceiling and reverberates in the large room.

"I would prefer not to, your highness. But if I may?" I dare to peek up at her.

The Queen's red eyes flash. She gathers her skirts in one hand and prances to her seat without answering me. Wren nudges me from behind with the edge of his boot, his face a mask of serenity. Panicking, I look to Altair who offers a hand. Taking it, I rise and walk hesitantly to the petulant ruler. She's already pawing at a small fox in her lap, disregarding me as I approach.

Deciding to act, I gather a bundle of my hair and motion to the Queen's lap. She pauses her attention and the fox tries to huddle into a ball to protect itself. Paused with my hands full of hair, I wait. Finally she motions for a servant to grab the small animal. Once her lap is free, I place my hair down. With a second armful, I kneel and wrap my locks around her, hoping nothing bad happens to me.

With my voice cracking out of fear, I hum until my hair glows, bathing the Queen in a heavenly shimmer. The light lasts longer than I've ever encountered and I lose my breath trying to maintain the incantation. After what feels like forever, I stop, almost collapsing.

"Is that it?" The Queen's shrill voice cuts through the silence like a knife. "Will I bear a child?"

"Your Highness, it is difficult to say. This magic is not mine to control. Only time will tell," I confess."But I have never seen my hair stay lit for so long."

She raises her hand and slaps me across the cheeks before I can react. All at once, Wren steps forward and drags me from the throne room. Behind us, the Queen begins throwing things and screaming incoherently. Shakily, I find my footing and begin following Wren out of the palace.

"This will not end well if she is not healed, Zelle." Wren bristles as we cross the courtyard.

"I don't know what I can do about that," I stutter. "I'm not a witch, I don't even know if it helped."

"Yes, I am aware. Something in my gut tells me your magic will not work for this task." Wren stops, staring into my eyes.

"And she will kill me?" I ask, frantic.

"Aye," Wren nods, his hands clenching mine. "I can't let that happen. I stalled having her call for you as long as I could. Now, you'll have to escape."

"Wait, you did what? I thought you hated me, all of

you Fae treat me so poorly." I look around, realizing we're deep in the maze of bushes where no one can see.

Wren's brow creases with worry and he pulls me closer. "No, Zelle. I do not hate you, which is a sin to my people. The opposite is true, and if anyone ever found my duplicitousness, I would be killed along with you. I never meant to confess my love for you for your own safety, but I cannot allow you to be killed."

All I can do is stare. Wren? My mind blown, I open my mouth but find no words. Wren's pained look cuts deep into my heart and I inhale painfully. "What now?"

"Now, your fight begins," a familiar voice cackles from behind us.

Wren and I both spin around and step backward as a young, beautiful version of Prax approaches. Her skin is no longer withered, her long, blonde hair covers her naked body just barely as she leads my unicorn through the maze toward us. Behind them I can just catch a glimpse of my other soldiers.

"What? Who are you?" Wren looks around with worry.

"This is the Goddess Prax," I hurry to explain. "She's here to help me."

"Ahh, youngling. My time is almost nigh. Here, my gift as promised," Prax interrupts, stepping between Wren and me. She lifts a lock of my hair and waves her arm around. A cloud of smoke appears and when it dissipates, she's holding a dagger. Blinking, I look from her palm to her serene face.

"Okay? What am I to do with such a small weapon," I ask, wincing at my forwardness.

Prax smiles and places the dagger in my hand. The hilt is engraved with flowers and I stare in wonder.

"It is not the size that matters, right, boys?" Prax giggles and Kain snorts. "The Sundrop dagger works in opposition to the magic you already possess. While the light of your hair gives life, the dagger will take life away with a mere pinprick. Those marked by this weapon will be doomed to roam the earth at night, soulless."

Trying to wrap my mind around what she is saying, I look at Xavier. His face is a mask, unreadable. Frustrated, I turn the weapon in my hands. It is light, but so heavy at the same time. As if the magic wants to pull me into the Earth.

Wren

I had been planning an escape for Zelle and I, but that is off the table now that there are more of us. How do you hide a unicorn? The two humanoids would be easier. At least those angel wings can be retracted into his skin.

The Goddess being in the realm, under my nose has me worrying more, what else is hiding here. But the only saving grace is that if I didn't know, then the King and Queen possibly wouldn't, either.

"Can we trust her?" I ask as we navigate more bushes.

"My heart tells me yes, and so far, it has yet to be wrong," Zelle replies.

"You were her jailer, and you doubt I'm trustworthy?" the regal woman asks.

"That I was, but I only did it so I could watch out for her. If I didn't, some other Fae would and they wouldn't have been as kind as I," I state matter of factly.

Kain neighs and knocks me in the back with his snout. If the Queen knew he was still on the grounds, she'd snatch him up right quick. We thought him lost.

"Yes, there were times I had to be more cruel than I would have liked to be, but it was a guise. If I didn't they would have been replacing me with a guard that would," I defend myself.

"I can verify that he was nicer than most, if a bit distant," Zelle adds.

"Where are we headed?" the fallen one asks.

"There's a little hut I've been stocking up for an escape. We can stay there. It's only supplied for two, but we can stretch it for the night," I scratch my head trying to remember what I have hoarded.

"We need weapons," Flynn speaks up for the first time since our little band started on our way. "From what I've seen, this place is well guarded, only a fool would try and get out unarmed."

"Let's just reach the cabin and we can talk more there. We need to be stealthy and not attract attention," I remind them. Not that we don't stick out like an eyesore, but at least if we are quiet it may look like I'm escorting the group somewhere.

"Wren?" Altair asks, his voice freezing me in my tracks. "Where are you and these prisoners headed? They belong in the dungeons."

I stumble over my words, trying to think of a good reason. Without hesitation, Zelle steps towards Altair and stabs him in the heart with her newly acquired dagger. The spot where she struck him begins to spill green blood, but not just that, his whole body shudders and he starts to throw up, expelling more green liquid.

"What is happening to him?" I gasp.

"Did you not hear my words?" the Goddess asks, "I told you all that the dagger takes life. It doesn't just kill, it changes them into a creature of the night."

"So, will he try to eat us? Should we keep moving?" Xavier questions.

"He will not harm Zelle, the rest of you, I can't be sure," Prax says.

"On we go," Flynn pipes in.

As much as I hate to leave Altair in that condition, my loyalty lies with Zelle now. If he does change and attack, I will not be any help to her if I'm dead. I mean I have no illusions that I may die getting her to safety, but Altair won't be the one to take my life.

"Follow me," I say, grabbing Zelle's hand and pulling her along.

This time, they follow me with no noise. I think that the run in with Altair and the effects of the dagger has everyone's minds spinning. This day has certainly taken a turn toward the impossible.

We walk for ten minutes, each step taking us closer to the hut.

"How much farther?" Prax speaks up.

"Are you well?" Zelle asks, face full of concern.

"No, it's nearing my time, but I want to see you to a safe place before I depart," the now old woman answers.

Zelle looks as if she wants to say something profound but no words come from her lips. Tears well in her eyes.

"Don't cry for me, I have had a long life. It's my time

and you will be a worthy successor," Prax says, wiping moisture from Zelle's cheek.

"Thank you," is all she can squeak out.

"We are almost there," I interrupt. "It won't be long and you can say your goodbyes there."

Both women nod at me and we continue a few feet.

"Well, this is a shit hole," Flynn comments.

"I did say it was a hut and I told you it was meant for two," I say, rolling my eyes at him before turning to Zelle. "What are we going to do about the unicorn? There will not be room for him inside with us."

"Not a problem, do you happen to have an extra pair of trousers?" she asks before whirling around to Kain.

"I do," I say disappearing into the shack, not sure I'm ready for whatever is about to happen.

When I emerge, Zelle is petting Kain and whispering into his ear.

"Will you toss me those?" she asks.

As soon as I release the fabric, the unicorn shifts into a man. Almost stumbling over my feet, I clasp my chest in surprise. It's the same man that was caught outside Zelle's tower.

"You knew he could shift?" I look at Zelle with my eyes wide.

"I did, but it wasn't my secret to spill." She shrugs.

"I am the last of my kind and I asked her not to tell. The Queen was the one that ordered not only my family to be killed but all of my kind. So, there is no telling what she would do to me if she found out."

I remember that campaign and I was one of the soldiers sent to slaughter the poor creatures. We weren't given a reason, just the mission, but I wasn't going to tell him that.

"Your secret is safe with me," I tell him honestly.

He gives me a little nod as he begins stepping into the pants. Mind blown for the second time this evening, I nod and head into the small hut. Behind me, Flynn and Xavier enter. The one room isn't much, but there's a table and two small cots along with the supplies I've gathered to take us across Faerie.

"Well, here we are. I hope you have a good plan, or we're all toast." Flynn turns one of the chairs around and sits.

"Flynn, be nice. Whatever Wren had planned probably won't suffice as I don't plan on leaving the Queen alive."

Every head turns quickly in her direction. "What?" Kain all but growls.

"You heard me. I can't allow her to continue ruining this realm. Not when I have the power to stop her. How many more creatures will come to extinction if I don't? It isn't right. She's evil."

"Zelle," I cross the room and take her hand. "You can't be serious. To take on the Queen would be suicide."

She wrenches away from me and tucks her body in the crook of the angel's wing. He fans them out, covering her. They whisper for a few moments while the rest of us look on with wonder. Seeing an angel this close is something no creature should take lightly. I was aghast when he arrived in our prison.

Kain leans against the wall, his eyes boring a hole in the floor. As much time as he spent being healed by Zelle, it's no wonder she's taken him as her own. I can smell him all over her and it makes me more jealous than I'd like to admit.

"So, what was your plan?" Flynn kicks a chair toward me.

I sit down, setting my bow next to me. "I had planned to trek across Faerie to the border on the North. The land there is inhabited by wolf shifters that had agreed to help me escape in exchange for freeing one of their wolf pups a few weeks back. I have already made good on my part.

"How far into Faerie are we talking?"

"Two days by foot," I sigh. "If we cross the nearest border, the Queen's spies will find us before our second step.

"Fair point. But now we have the added complication of Zelle's mission. Can it be done?"

"She and I can take down the Queen." Xavier's wings snap open and Zelle steps out glowing.

If we didn't have more serious matters to discuss, I would stare longer. But as it is, I can almost hear a clock ticking in the back of my mind. "Tell us how," I demand.

"Wren, you will take Xavier and I before the Queen. You will tell her we have a plan that might heal her womb. From there we trick her into seeing us alone. I will stab her and Xavier will fly us up through the glass dome to safety. The rest of you will need to wait outside the palace in the forest for us."

Staring at the determination on Zelle's face, I find myself at a loss for words. Playing the scene out in my head, I can't find fault in it—but still my gut won't settle. There's something they're missing.

"How many guards are in the palace?" Flynn asks, scowling at Xavier.

"A hundred, give or take. The Queen, alone, has twenty personal guards, plus the King's fifty and any that are on patrol. All will kill first." I sigh, playing with the numbers in my head. Even if we could get the Queen alone, the alert would sound fast if she were killed.

"Zelle, I don't feel good about this at all. There has to be another way. Can't we plant a Goddess bomb or something easier?" Kain points toward the quickly withering Goddess. "What if your hair trips you, as it does. So many things could go wrong."

The Goddess taps on the ground with her cane. "I cannot explode at will, young unicorn. I can solve the problem of Zelle's hair. Once I infuse the last of my power into the dagger, she may use it to cut her locks without risking their magic. Only the blade of the Sundrop dagger can do this work. If you truly feel you must carry out this deed, I will also pray to my mother, the Goddess of Strength, to help you at your task."

"It is good enough for me." Zelle kneels in front of the woman.

A blinding light flashes and I cover my eyes. When I move my hand, the Goddess is gone and Zelle is standing. Her blonde hair lay in mounds around her, only enough to flow past her waist left behind. She looks pointedly at each one of us. Her stare has a way of making me feel both large and small at the same time. I knew from the moment I laid eyes on Zelle that I would move mountains for her if I could. Now is my chance to prove as much.

"We should rest tonight. The Queen weakens in the morning as she sleeps fitfully. Let me get you some pants, running in that dress will only slow you down," I turn and begin to rummage in the chests.

"Then it's settled. Let's eat and rest for the night," Zelle's voice catches. The pain in those words almost tears me apart. When I turn toward her, she's deep in the embrace of Kain's arms. Heart aching, I resume my search. Will there be room in her heart for me as well?

Xavier's wing brushes against my shoulder and I look over. "She finds something redeemable in Flynn," he chuckles. "Don't worry about your standing with her. She's not like any female I've seen in my millennia of life.

A wave of relief washes over me. I would ask how he is certain, but the guy is an angel. I figure he knows better than I. My heart a little lighter, I finally come across one of the female scout outfits I stored for Zelle. The clothing in hand, I stand.

"Here, this will work better for our purposes," I hand the pile to her. "Do you want us to step out?"

"Why? All here have seen me naked already." Zelle shrugs and loosens her gown. It falls to the floor and I almost fall backward. With the grace of a Goddess, she stands nude and glowing as brightly as her hair during a healing.

"Well, lass, hopefully you won't do that in bed. I don't know if I can work under such duress," Flynn guffaws and we all begin to laugh.

Zelle

I awaken to angel wings on top of me acting as a blanket. Caressing the one closest to my hand, I watch as Xavier moves back from me with a smile on his face.

"Morning," he says before removing his wing from me.

I shudder a little at the loss of his warmth even though it's not really cold in Faerie. Do you want me to put it back?" he questions.

"Oh," my cheeks flush, "I'm fine."

He winks before standing and exiting this little hut. I get up and follow, but stop at the door to watch as Xavier extends his wings. I marvel at his wingspan, which I hadn't really noticed until now.

"Well, that will be hard to compete with," Flynn whispers in my ear.

I jump a little before replying. "Jealous?"

"Do I look like a guy that needs to be?" he questions.

"Yeah, yeah you do," I smirk, turning towards him.

"Ouch, Blondie," he states with a hand over his heart.

The back and forth between Flynn and I has become a thing, I realize. With a laugh, I turn away from him and glance toward Wren. The guard is in the far corner of the hut rifling through some sacks.

"Wren?" I query.

"Hmm?" he says with a piece of dried meat in his mouth.

"Should we head to the castle? Start the plan?" I ask. I know that he isn't happy about killing the Queen, but if he really cares for me as he says, then he should go along with it, right?

He nods and hands me a piece of the jerky, "Sorry, I don't have anything other than dried meats and fruits. I thought we were going to be on the run and they are easy to pack."

I bite a chunk off, chewing and swallowing with zest. I hadn't realized how hungry I was. "It's perfect."

This gets a little grin from him, his teeth full of bits from his breakfast. I smile back but don't tell him about his teeth. We have a plan to carry out and it may be a death sentence, but I know in my heart that I can't leave here with that hag on the throne.

"So, do you think we will run into Altair?" Wren asks, running a hand through his hair.

"Prax said a creature of the night, I'm not entirely sure what that means, but I don't think we will have to worry about him in the daylight," I pause before continuing, "and I'm sorry that I had to change him."

Wren holds up a hand to stop me. "He was as close to a best friend as I have ever had, but he was close to the Queen. She's pure evil. It's best that you did. I was not lying when I pledged myself to you. I pick you. So, there are no hard feelings. I just wish you would listen and just leave this place. Let me bring you back to the mortal realm. Get you back to your true family."

"I will. But not until after this Queen is dead," I promise. "I have no intention of ruling this realm but she doesn't deserve to, either."

This time, Kain speaks up, for the first time this morning, "I want revenge, The Queen is the reason that my whole family, hell the entire unicorn-shifter race is dead. Still, dread fills me at the thought of your plan, Zelle. I have a feeling we aren't going to make it out."

For the first time, I'm speechless. I am fully aware that we probably won't get out of the castle unharmed but death was never a thought that crossed my mind.

"I...uh...," I start.

"If Zelle says we are killing the Queen, that's what we do," Xavier pipes up from the doorway. "Evil people shouldn't be placed in places of power. If we can change that, why wouldn't we?"

"There is always another one waiting to take their place. How can we assure the people of this realm that their next leader isn't just as bad or worse?" Kain asks.

"We can't but we can remove this one. I know not all Fae are bad," I say, my gaze moving toward Wren.

"Are we ready?" Wren asks, shutting down the conversation. "The Queen will be up and around soon to start her day of torture. She may be ill, but that doesn't stop her."

"Yes, let's go," I say, before I can back out.

Before I leave, I cross the room to grab the dagger from where I hid it. As I reach down, Kain grabs my wrist.

"Do you really have to do this?" Kain pleads, hazel eyes boring into mine.

"I do." I purse my lips.

He sighs but releases me. "Fine, Flynn and I will pack what we can and be ready on the north side of the castle. If things go bad, know that I will not wait in the trees, I will come in and fight. If I am destined to die, it will be because I'm fighting to save you."

I pull him close, "It will not come to that," I vow before placing my lips on his.

"Don't make promises you can't keep," he says, moving away from me.

I know he is right to be angry, but I'm determined that we all survive and live happily ever after. The Queen will fall this day and Faerie will be allowed a fresh start without her grasp. This is if King Thayer doesn't continue her evil.

Kain doesn't say anything else. I watch as he crosses the small room with a frown on his beautiful face. He kneels and joins Flynn who is rifling through what Wren has gathered. My heart is a little sad that he could so easily turn from me, but I know that it's only that he can't agree with the plan and this was his way to deal with it all.

"Ready?" Wren asks.

"Will the Queen see me in pants? Or should I have a dress on?" I ask.

"Let's pull your hair up, but the pants will be fine. I just pray she doesn't notice that your hair is shorter than it was yesterday," Wren says.

Shit, I didn't think about that when I let Prax cut it with the dagger but I know that it was for the best.

"Maybe you could wear a cloak?" Flynn stands, handing me one that is deep red.

With a nod I take it and wrap the fabric around my shoulders. Before pulling up the hood, I pull my hair back and wrap a strand around it to keep it out of my face. It's the best I can do for now without braiding it. This time I grab the dagger and tuck it into my pants to help conceal it.

"Let's go," I stare at Wren and Xavier before I can back out.

As I cross the threshold of the small hut, I look back at Kain and Flynn. It pains me to part from them, but I whisper a little prayer for their safety all the same. For all of our safety. Let the Goddess be with us.

Wren looks regal in the sunshine with his bow over one shoulder and his green cloak draped perfectly. Looking from him to Xavier, I take a deep breath. Hopefully, this is the start of something and not the end. My soldiers deserve a better life than the one that has been given.

"Lead the way." I gulp as I wave toward Wren. He looks me over before turning on a heel and marching toward the palace.

Following behind the guard is something familiar. Holding onto that, I clasp Xavier's hand and hum the healing incantation. It doesn't hurt to make sure both of us are tip-top before this little expedition begins in earnest.

"I love the way it feels when your magic touches mine. I don't understand it, but I love it," Xavier whispers.

"Have you ever loved a human?" I ask.

"A few. But none compare to you, Zelle."

"You got that right. From one old soul to another, we found a diamond in the rough." Wren smiles over his shoulder. "Now, no more talking. We're entering the grounds."

It seems as soon as Wren spoke of being quiet, nature decided to play tricks on us. Every branch and leaf we step on seems to scream "here we are." Wincing, I try to tiptoe to no avail. Thankfully, we leave the forest and step onto the soft moss of the courtyard. Winding through the maze, we close the distance between us and the castle.

"Wren, why are you at the palace so early? the doorman asks.

"These two have urgent news for the Queen. I seek an audience immediately," Wren stares the Fae down with quiet authority.

"Very well. You know the way. She's in her garden taking tea."

Wren nods, then waves for us to follow. My heart is in my throat as I listen to his feet hit the marble ahead of us. Unwittingly, I pat my side. The blade feels unnatural as it bores into my flesh. At the same time, I am comforted knowing I have the power of a Goddess at my fingertips.

"Steady," Wren warns before stopping at a large, white door. He looks to me, eyes creased with worry before pushing it open. "My Queen," Wren bows. "I come with news. These two prisoners think they've got a solution to what ails you." He ushers us forward with mock force.

Xavier and I kneel before the Queen. I stare at the floor, waiting for her to reply. There's a tapping, which I can only assume is her nails on the small table as we wait. Her slippered feet poke out from beneath a cream-colored gown. I stare at the gold thread that binds them, trying my best not to fall apart.

"What is this news, human?" the Queen's lacquered nail scrapes the bottom of my chin.

I look up into her red eyes and my throat dries. Here goes nothing. "Your highness, the power that I have is small compared to that of an angel. This fallen one cannot access many of his powers in Faerie, but I believe we can combine our magics. Essentially, his Godly power would strengthen my healing power and enable me to fight what is ailing your womb."

The Queen purses her lips. She looks from Xavier to me and back again before she rises. "Everyone OUT!" she screams and relief hits me like a punch in the gut.

One part of our plan is already done. Add that to the fact that we are in her small garden and Xavier should have no problem getting us out. I almost hyperventilate thinking about what I must do next, but one look at Wren gives me the strength I need to calm down.

The guards quickly scurry, as well as the handmaids surrounding the Queen. In moments, the garden is still but for the sound of the Queen's nails tapping on the table. Trying to remain serene, I wait for my opportunity.

"It seems worth a try, does it not?" Wren asks from his position beside me.

Moments tick by with no answer, but I cannot bring myself to look into her red eyes again. Instead, I stare at the flagstone beneath me as if it might hold the wonders of time.

"Indeed. Tell me how this will work," she finally replies.

"If you could lay on that chaise lounge," Xavier's voice startles me. "I will stand behind the girl as she works her magic. I will imbue mine by touching her shoulder."

"Very well," the Queen stands and crosses the garden to lay down on a pink lounge surrounded by roses.

Sweat breaks out on my upper lip as I rise, stomach in knots. Slowly, the three of us walk toward the Queen. Careful not to show anything but the usual fear I have for the royals, I kneel. She doesn't even look at me. Her head is turned toward a large rose. Her fingers pull the bud to her nose and I take the opportunity to pull out the dagger. Before I can second guess myself, I reach over and slice her neck from ear to ear. Blood gushes forth and her eyes open with surprise.

It is in that moment that I feel her fire energy bursting out of her wildly. Before the flame hits me in the face, Xavier has wrapped his arms around me and vaulted us into the air. A faint moment of fear hits me, thinking we left Wren; but when I look down, he is nowhere below.

Zelle

"What's with the smoke?" Flynn asks.

"As the Queen bled to death she called upon her fire magic to try and burn us," Wren states. "After I lopped off her head, Xavier grabbed Zelle and I leapt on his back just in the nick of time to get out of the flames."

"Good thing you had the fallen angel, huh?" Flynn questions.

"Yeah, I wasn't expecting that," I say honestly. "Why didn't I know that she had fire powers?"

Wren gulps, "Most Fae aren't in touch with their elemental magic, as long as I've served in the castle, I've never seen or heard of her using her powers."

Kain moves closer to me, "We need to move, this is talk for later."

"You're right." I say, caressing his cheek. "After we land in the human realm, I want to find Gothel. She, too, must pay the price for her misdeeds."

Heads nod in agreement and Wren steps to the front of the group. Flynn hands me a pack, I slide it over my shoulder and tangle my fingers with Kain.

Without a word, Wren leads us into the cover of the thick forest. Flynn and Xavier flank Kain and I, ever vigilant.

"Would you like me to shift? You and Flynn can ride and we could cover more ground," Kain offers.

"That's sweet of you to offer, but let's wait. I know we're on the run, but it's been too long since I got to walk free. If there is a call for a quick escape, I will take you up on your offer." I smile.

"Could we at least pick up the pace?" Kain's face is scrunched with worry. My heart pains to see him so jumpy.

I squeeze his hand for assurance. "I think that's doable."

"Wren, do you know where you are going?" Flynn calls from behind us.

"Yes. I've taken this route a few times in preparation. It has always been my intention to save Zelle. I only acted harshly to her to cover up my true nature and keep her safe," Wren states without stopping.

"How far is the northern border?" Xavier asks.

"Two day's walk," Wren almost whispers.

"Did we pack any water?" I ask, knowing that hydrating is imperative.

"There are a couple brooks and a stream on the route." Wren answers. He pauses before continuing, "We better stop talking. We need to keep our ears open in case we are being followed or if there are any guards on our tail."

Wren is right, of course, but I can't stop my mind from spinning. Instead of asking more questions, I zip my lips and decide to enjoy the greenery around us. Most would take a walk in the forest for granted, but this is a treat I've only been able to enjoy a handful of times in my life.

As much as I long to simply just roll around in the lush grass I don't. I hate that my first glimpse of freedom is so rushed, but I remind myself that I just killed the Queen. We aren't safe. Even with as horrible as she was, the King will still call for my head. It's best that we leave the realm quickly.

My feet start to ache, it's been a while since I have been on a trek like this but I push on. There are a couple times I think of asking Kain to shift but I don't want to weigh him down. I breathe a sigh of relief when Wren stops at the first little brook.

With a sigh of contentment, I take a seat under a shade tree and begin to rub my aching feet.

"Are you okay, Zelle?" Xavier asks, kneeling next to me.

"Yes, I'm fine. My feet are just sore from all the walking. Nothing I can't handle," I assure him.

"Does your hair work on yourself?" he asks as he arches an eyebrow at me.

"Yes, but healing also takes some of my energy," I reply. "It works differently than when I heal someone else."

"We still have a long distance to cover today, it may be worth it to try," he advises me.

"I'll think about it," I promise.

My fake mother had always told me that my hair's powers were to help others and not myself. Sure, I've

143

used it selfishly a handful of times, but for some reason I'm hesitant just now. Maybe I'm afraid of how I might have changed now that Prax's magic is blended with my own.

Wren brings over a bowl of fresh water, "Drink, we need to get moving soon."

I thank him wordlessly, accepting the liquid. Without another thought, I drink it all down in one gulp.

"May I have more?"

He smiles and returns back to the stream to refill the bowl.

"Thank you," I smile. Standing to take the bowl from him, I wobble a little on my tired legs. "I was more parched than I thought."

Once I drink the liquid down, Wren takes the bowl and returns it to his pack.

"Time to get moving, I have a bad feeling we're being tracked." Wren's head snaps up as a twig cracks behind us.

The four men scramble, grabbing packs and ushering me across the water. Xavier and Wren whisper, heads together as Kain and Flynn grab my arms and all but whisk me away. My head is spinning, there's no telling what's behind us but I can't bring myself to look.

"Over here!" Wren calls, waving at what seems to be a pile of brush. He grabs at the group, pulling up a trap door. Without asking, I barrel through the opening. Quick as a flash, the group follows. We're almost hidden when an arm catches the door.

"Stop, by order of the King!" A familiar voice shouts and my heart sinks. I'd hoped to get away with only killing the two I left behind, but it looks like fate has other plans for us.

"How could you betray your sovereign?" Cavill wrenches Wren from the dugout.

The two square off, all but growling at each other giving the four with the guard time to close in on us. My heart thunders beneath my breastbone as I try to decide what to do. My mind is made up when Cavill punches Wren in the jaw, sending him to the ground with a sickening thud.

"Get your mitts off him!" I yell as I take a step out of the darkness, dagger raised.

"Princess," Cavill chuckles. "Of course, it was you who led him astray. I told the King this would happen, but he was also blinded by your pretty face," he spits at Wren's boots.

My blood boils. Taking a step toward him, I purse my lips. Cavill isn't even paying attention, his head is turned as he barks orders to his men which gives me the perfect opportunity to slide my blade into his side. I'm surprised at how easy it is to pierce through his leathers and deep into his meat. Cavill roars with pain and drops to the ground holding the wound.

After stepping away from Cavill, I realize I'm surrounded by absolute chaos. My men are engaged with the other soldiers in an all-out brawl. Worried about Cavill changing, as we don't know the timeframe for the Dagger's magic, I tiptoe around the fight, trying to find a way to help. When the opportunity arises, I stab another soldier in the side. I continue my dance around the fighting men, aiming for our attackers when their backs are turned toward me.

The last pair fighting are Kain and a female Fae. She scratches her fingers across Kain's chest and it's all I can do not to rip her head off. Stepping up behind her, I grab her head and slit her throat to the bone. Her body hits the ground with a squelch and Kain is left staring at me wide-eyed.

"Cavill is twitching, we'd better get out of here fast." Wren struggles to a stand.

"I'll carry Wren and Flynn. Xavier, you should fly with Zelle. Follow us as Wren knows the way," Kain barks as his body wavers. He rips off his pants just before the shift, throwing them at Flynn.

No one argues. The two males hop onto Kain's back and Xavier sweeps me off my feet. Wind whooshes around us as Xavier flaps his beautiful wings. This time, our ascent is more controlled and my belly doesn't do somersaults on the way up. Kain's muscular unicorn gallops across the plain effortlessly, even carrying my two strong males.

Craning my neck, I can see the bodies we left behind begin to flop around. Hopefully, the sun will keep them down long enough for us to put some distance between us. Hoping against hope, I send a prayer to the heavens. *Anyone who can hear me, please let us find safety.*

The green landscape seems to go on and on forever. I can tell Xavier is tiring by the way he dips a little lower every few moments. Worried, I look up trying to catch the angel's eye.

"If Kain doesn't don't stop soon, I'll swoop lower," he tangles a hand in my hair, reassuring me. "Don't worry, Zelle, I would never drop you."

"I know you are tiring, do you think you can push a little bit and stop in front of them?" I question my angel. "Or you could even set me down and stop them, that way my weight isn't slowing you down."

"I'm not leaving you in those woods alone," he says.

"I'm not alone, I have the dagger," I counter. "Besides, the undead will not attack me, so it's only the living I have to watch out for."

He sighs and that tells me that he knows I'm right. I watch as he scans the forest floor below us. Xavier doesn't speak again until he finds what his eyes were scanning for.

"I'll set you down by the stream there." Xavier points.

I turn to see where he means and I nod to tell him I understand. He starts his descent and gently sets me on a boulder near the water.

"I will be back for you, but if you hear anything heading in your direction I want you to go upstream and find a hiding place. Do you understand?" he asks.

I nod.

"Promise me," he states, his mouth a firm line.

"I promise. You really need to get back in the air before Kain gets farther ahead," I remind him.

"I'm going, but if you are hiding, I'll whistle like

this," he says before making a little noise with his lips. "Only then are you to come out of hiding."

"Got it, now please get going," I tell him. I hate sending him on without me but I know it's the only way that he can head off Kain.

I watch as he returns to the sky and I don't look away until he is no more than a little speck. With any luck Xavier will get to Kain before he is too far ahead. Scanning around, I realize that this might be a good place to make camp for the night. I start to look around for a suitable place that the five of us can rest, but not straying too far from the stream where Xavier left me. I certainly don't want him thinking something happened to me if he can't find me when he returns.

Zelle

There is a crack of a branch behind me and I duck behind the nearest row of bushes. Not the best hiding place but I did tell Xavier I wouldn't stay in the open. I do what I can to stay disguised in the bush yet peek at the same time. I can't see the whole clearing from where I am, but I can make out a shadowy figure in the tree line on the other side.

The figure moves closer, stopping just out of the sun's rays. With care, the human shape steps one foot into the light, as if testing it. With bated breath, I watch as it tests a few more times before the changed Cavill moves forward. It's obvious he's being careful to keep his exposed skin under the shade of the trees.

"Come out, Zelle," he orders.

I suppress the squeal that threatens to escape my throat, not replying to the monster I had a hand in creating.

"I can smell you, Princess. You have nothing to fear, I will not harm you," he promises.

I remember Prax saying the creatures the dagger

creates can't harm me, but I don't know if I want to test her words.

"Step into the sun, let me see all of you," I order.

"Can't," he grits out as he moves one hand into the light. Smoke rises from his skin and he pulls it back into the shadows. I watch as he struggles with my command. He has a strong will but my words win and he fully emerges into the light.

Standing behind the bushes I gasp in horror as more smoke rises and he begins to scream. I don't understand why he is standing there in agony. *Unless he has to do what I say?*

"Return to the shade!" I shout. This time he complies without hesitation. "Why do you obey me?" I step out of my hiding.

"You made me what I am, so I must obey. The dagger you hold changed me but also made me yours to command, it whispers to me. I didn't want to follow you, but the compulsion was too much to resist." He shrugs.

That's weird, I was aware I would create creatures of the night, but not that they would follow me and my orders.

"If that's true, there are at least two more that were marked with this dagger, where are they?" I look around suddenly uneasy. I'm like a homing beacon, and the thought of that is creepy.

Before I can blink, Altair and the Fae whose throat I slit step beside Cavill. Shit, what am I going to do with them? I can't have them harming my men.

"And if I told you to stop following me, would you do that?" I ask.

"If that is your command, then we will," Cavill answers for the three of them.

"What if I ask for you to help me get out of this realm and to kill any who try to harm me? Can you control yourselves?" I ask.

"If that is your command," Cavill repeats.

"Zelle?" Kain's voice floats near the clearing.

"Hide and do not harm the men that are coming to me," I order.

The three vampires nod and disappear into the cover of the trees.

Lump in my throat, I untangle myself from the bushes and walk back toward the stream before calling out. "I'm here."

All four men run over to me, smiles on their lips.

"Where were you?" Kain asks as he pulls me in close.

"Hiding," I admit honestly. "Xavier made me promise to hide if I heard any noise."

"What did you hear?" Wren asks, moving closer to me.

"A branch break," I tell him.

"Is there someone out there?" Flynn asks.

"You are all so full of questions, aren't you?" I try to avoid the question versus lie.

"Was there, Zelle?" Xavier asks.

The tone in his voice stabs me right in the heart. There's no way I can hide anything from my angel.

151

"Yes, three vampires I created. They didn't harm me and will not harm you," I say quickly.

"How do you know that?" Kain questions, raising a brow at me.

"I had a little talk with them," I squeak out.

Anger crosses all their faces. "You did what?" Xavier asks.

"It's Cavill, Altair, and that female Fae. They are bound to me by the dagger. Whatever I order, they do and I told them not to hurt anyone that doesn't hurt me," I tell them. "I swear I had no idea this would happen." I wring my hands.

"Zelle, what the hell? You could have died!"

"But I didn't. Please, don't treat me as if I'm some fragile thing. I didn't call them, they found me. I hid until I realized what was going on. There's nothing for it now, they are here. I could banish them or we can use them as weapons."

Wren steps up, his face a mask of pain. "If we can use them as weapons, I say we do it. Who knows what the King will throw our way. I don't like it, but we have to protect ourselves in any way possible."

With a few huffs and puffs, the other two men give in. "Fine," Xavier grits. "But as soon as we don't need them, you get rid of them. It's unnatural." He shivers.

My shoulders relax and I nod. "I'm going to task them with keeping watch. We need to rest, especially Xavier," I speak over my shoulder as I leave the circle.

Making my way back to my hiding spot, I grumble inwardly. The price of freedom seems to get steeper by the minute, I really hope the fates will leave the cost alone after this. I wish my life were easier, maybe after this?

"Cavill?" I call out.

"I am here," Cavill taps on the tree that he's hiding behind. All three vampires step around it with a speed that's almost dizzying. The female drops a mangled bunny and wipes blood from her face with her sleeve. I shudder and freeze in my tracks.

"What the—?" I stare with my mouth open.

Cavill slaps the female before turning fully toward me. "We crave fresh blood now. It is a gnawing need."

Awesome. I was only half kidding when I branded them vampires. I didn't know they were actually going to be blood suckers. Sheesh. "Okay, the blood of my men is off limits. You three are not to touch a hair on their heads unless it's to save them from harm. Am I clear?"

"Your previous command was already sufficient." Cavill bows dramatically.

"Good. I need you to spread out and keep watch while we rest. I don't want to see you lurking around, be discreet. As much as it pains me to have created and now command you—it's also creepy. I don't know how to release you from this life, but if it is your wish, I will help you once we have our freedom."

"Very well, Princess." Cavill nods and they disappear into the foliage.

Everything seems to be happening so fast. Most of my life has been spent isolated, waiting for something. Now my head is spinning and my heart won't slow with the anticipation of freedom. Is it too much to ask to be happy?

"Why the long face, Blondie?" The softness in Flynn's voice catches me by surprise. I hadn't noticed him leaning against the tree. Looking into his deep-brown eyes, my heart skips a beat. Without a word, he crosses the small space between us and folds me in his arms. The hug turns out to be exactly what I needed.

"Thank you." I nestle my face in the crook of his neck.

Flynn's arms tighten around me. I can feel his heart thumping beneath my hand. For a moment we stand in silence but for the rustling of the leaves. A sense of peace washes over me and I tip my head to look at him. Our eyes meet and I bite my lip.

"Blondie," Flynn starts, then wraps a hand around my neck and places his full lips against mine. The kiss is as tender as a rose blossom. As quickly as it began, it ends leaving me feeling unsatisfied when Flynn brushes his thumb over my bottom lip.

"We will have time for this later. Please be careful with your creatures, Zelle. We've all just found you and none want to lose you," Flynn whispers, his voice cracking at the end. My eyes fill with tears. Flynn kisses the wet trail on my cheek, takes my hand and leads me to the little stream. Without a word he pulls out a square of fabric, dips it in the water and uses it to clean my face. Not used to him without an attitude, I stand there gawking like a fool.

"Come on and join the group. We need to eat and

rest, as you commanded." Flynn pins me with his signature wink.

A small giggle bubbles up and I let it out. Before I know it, I am full-belly laughing and I have no idea why.

"What's going on?" Kain runs over. "Did Flynn try to show you his tiny member?"

"Har Har, stallion, just because we've all seen what you're packing." Flynn playfully slaps Kain on the back.

Kain blushes then grabs my hand and leads me over to the small fire Wren is standing over. Xavier has a small rabbit skewered on a stick and is turning the meat in the flames. My mouth waters at the smell of food.

"I'll get some water," Flynn grabs a bowl from the pack and returns to the stream.

Wanting to be useful, I dig in the packs until I find the sleeping rolls. Laying them out gives me something to do with my hands while I sort through my feelings. I may be naive, but I think I love all of these men. Each for a different reason. Kain has been my constant, my first intimacy. Xavier has a strength in him that makes me feel safe. Wren snuck into my soul when I wasn't paying attention and then there's Flynn. The pretty boy who hides behind humor. I bet he just needs to be loved.

"Penny for your thoughts?" Wren touches my shoulder lightly.

My face flushes and I smile. "Oh nothing really. Is the food ready?" Wren's eyebrow rises and he nods. Not wanting to get all in my feelings, I touch his cheek

ROWAN THALIA & JENÉE ROBINSON

before walking over to Xavier who is dishing out the meal.

"Can I help?"

"Sure, just divide the berries into the bowls," Xavier answers. "I can feel your emotions, by the way. It's only happened to me once before, but I thought you should know since it feels so personal."

Blinking, I stare at him. His cheeks color and his eyes flare golden. Yes, it is love. Everything in me wants to ask him to fold me in his wings and hold me close. But I don't, I stand there remembering the softness of the feathers brushing against my face wishing we were far far away from this realm.

Xavier

Our meal was short and uneventful. I kept an eye on Zelle, I know she trusts the unholy creatures but I do not. In the human realm, the masters were cold and calculating, they didn't keep their creations from torturing or murdering the innocent. In fact, that was their favorite prey.

"Xavier," Zelle's voice brings me back to reality. "Are you good with the plan?"

I didn't hear a word of what they were saying. "Hmm?"

That gets the four of them to laugh.

Zelle stops and clears her throat, "We are going to take shifts sleeping. You and Wren are up first, are you good with that?"

I nod. What she doesn't know is that angels don't sleep. When she slept on me, I just laid next to her to keep her warm.

"Great." She smiles and starts to clean up dinner.

"I will clean up, you three get some rest," I offer.

Zelle steps over to where I'm perched on a rock and kisses me lightly on my lips. "Be careful," she whispers before moving toward Wren. Instead of kissing his lips, she brushes a hand though his long hair and kisses his cheek. The gentle way she treats us both separately makes my heart swell.

There is no jealousy rising up in me as I expect there would be. In the beginning, it was clear that Wren was the enemy. Now I'm on the fence as to whether he can be trusted or not.

I don't move from my spot until Zelle, Flynn, and Kain are in their sleeping bags. Standing, I stretch, after sitting for a little too long.

"I'm going to check the perimeter," I state over my shoulder..

Wren tosses me a sword, and gives me a nod. Before leaving, I grab a tree branch and create a torch. I don't really need the light for seeing, but the flame will be useful all the same.

"I come in peace," I announce to the monsters in the woods.

Cavill answers, "You are safe with us."

The husky tone in his voice makes a shiver run down my spine, but there is a ring of truth to his words.

"Thank you. I'm just checking the woods. My weapon is only for those that mean to harm us," I over explain.

"Altair will join you," Cavill points to the bushes. Altair jumps out of his hiding place.

"Appreciated." I tip my head to the former Queen's guard.

Altair follows without a word. Though I do notice

he stays near my darkened side, avoiding the flames of my torch. Angels are well known for being soundless and Altair is even lighter on his feet for his large size. We make a circle around the makeshift camp which doesn't take us long. I thank my companion for his help before he disappears once again.

"All is quiet," I report to Wren as I reenter the clearing and throw my dimming branch into the fire.

"And the others?" he asks, motioning into the woods.

"Standing guard," I reply.

"Good, Flynn's snores will scare animals away, but may attract the Fae," Wren complains.

"If it gets worse, we will wake him," I assure him, taking my seat once again.

"So, do you mind me asking how you got into the Fae realm?" Wren asks, sitting opposite of me.

"I was taken," I say flatly.

He arches a brow at me, "That seems to be the way most outsiders get here."

"Are all Fae wicked?" I question him this time.

"Most yes, it's just in our nature, but sick and twisted? Not at all. I was raised like a normal human child. Mother, Father, and a sister. Fae children are rare and that's why the Queen turned into the brute she was. Her one job was to produce an heir and she wouldn't stop until she got that. Not that that's a good reason to commit such atrocities," Wren backpedals a little.

"It's the same in the human realm," I comment. "I

fell from Heaven because my older brother is an asshole."

"How's that?" Wren asks.

"He is the hand of God and with that, he believes he is mightier than all of the angels. I stood up to him when he went to smite a human. I wouldn't allow him to do it and I was taken before an angel committee. They pushed for me to have my wings clipped and my powers taken, but to my surprise, my brother pushed for me just to live among the humans. It is a fitting punishment since I got in the way of his duties," I confess.

"Wow, that is a punishment. Here they would just behead you and move on," Wren tells me.

"And that's why there aren't many Fae. If children are so hard to come by, why kill them? You could just jail them or do as you do for all the prisoners from other places. Then your population wouldn't be dying out," I state.

"Well, I never said that our rulers were the brightest." Wren shrugs.

"Why were you a guard?" I query.

"There isn't an option for males not to be," he starts. "When you hit fifteen, you are enrolled into the guard. After ten years of service you can stay or leave. I worked my way up to guarding Zelle. There wasn't any way I could leave after gaining that assignment. Altair and I may have been gruff with her but if we showed favoritism at all we would have been reassigned. We both knew if that happened they would do more than bully her. There aren't many women in the prison, so we both knew we had to keep her from being abused," Wren explains.

I nod that I understand, sounds a lot like humans as well. We sit in silence for a long time. Wren starts to say something a few times but thinks better of it. Once the first rays of the sun start to peek over the trees, I realize that Wren and I let the other two men sleep too long.

"Should we wake them?" I ask Wren.

"Nah, I'm not tired at all," he says with a yawn.

I'm about to tell him to rest when Cavill steps just into sight but under the shade of the tree.

"Soldiers are nearing, You need to wake the others," he says flatly. The omission of emotion in the vampire's voice bristles my feathers.

In a flurry of movement, Wren and I shake everyone awake. The paleness of Zelle's face makes my stomach turn. I wish she didn't have to endure such terror all of her days. If there is any of my Father's grace left in me, I hope that I might make her life better when we have escaped this realm.

"Zelle, jump on Kain's back. The rest of us will fan out and keep them at bay while you gain ground. We'll meet you at the next river. There's a large cave near the waterfall. I've marked the path on the rock using this symbol," Wren draws a star with a crescent moon in the dirt.

"They will never stop," Zelle says flatly, refusing to mount the unicorn.

"It won't matter once we get to the human realm.

We can disappear," Wren pleads, looking from side to side.

"They tracked and captured Xavier once. What's to stop them from finding us again?" Zelle's voice is strained. "I don't want to run. We can't let King Thayer continue his rule. Nor should we leave the hundreds of prisoners behind."

Kain stomps his front hoof against the rocks in anger and I have to agree with him. "Zelle, we do not have the numbers to fight the King and we are running out of time. Please mount the unicorn and get to safety."

"We can do a sneak attack. It wouldn't take much to fly in and take out Thayer, then open the dungeon," Zelle suggests.

"This is a terrible decision. But if you say it must be, then it will be so." I take a knee in front of her.

"What if we ambush this next set of soldiers and make more of your creatures?" Flynn adds.

"Yes!" Zelle's eyes light up with an evil flicker that dries my throat. My eyes drift to the blade she cups at her chest and my blood runs cold. There's something about it that doesn't sit right with me but we will never win this fight without it.

"If this is what we're doing we must jump into the offensive now!" Wren growls. "Flynn choose your weapon and hide in the rock formation. I'll climb the trees above you with my bow. Kain, take Zelle on a wide arc and flank the soldiers so that the Princess can catch them from behind. Xavier, can you notify the creatures?"

Not happy, but also not willing to cost us more time, I nod and take flight. It's easy to pick the creatures out of the foliage, they have an ungodly glow about them that my eyes pick up immediately. Swooping low, I whistle.

"Zelle has decided to attack the soldiers. You are to help. She doesn't want them dead, she needs to recruit them with her dagger."

"Understood," the leader answers before rushing through the shadows toward the incoming Fae.

Unsure of my role outside of keeping an eye on the fray, I shoot toward the clouds. Once I spot Kain, I follow him. But not close enough that an arrow or Fae net can catch me a second time. My ego still smarts thinking about being ripped out of the sky by their magic.

It's one thing to be an outcast, but to have lost my freedom to such beings as the Fae is a slap in the face that won't be lightly forgotten. Perhaps my Father knew Zelle needed me here? If that's the case, I would endure it a thousand times again. Seeing her ride the unicorn sets my heart fluttering. Her long hair flows around her, framing a fierceness in her face that wasn't there before.

The small army tracking us appears as if out of nowhere. Taking a quick count, I number them at about fifty. Sending a prayer up, I anxiously watch as Kain circles wide. I don't know how he knows where the soldiers are, but his path is true. Once he is behind them, he turns and brings Zelle behind the lot.

Before Kain reaches the back of the arrow formation, the creatures have begun picking off the right. As the Fae walk into the shadows they drop. At first, I thought they were being killed against Zelle's wishes. But then I watched closely. The one called Cavill dropped one, then fed his blood to that Fae. After a few minutes, the same undead glow lit the Fae from within. Only the new light seems dimmer. As if the farther removed from the Goddess's dagger, the less magic flows into the creatures. Taking a mental note, I train my attention back to Zelle. By the time I pick her out of the landscape, she's ambushed three Fae, their lights as bright as Cavill's. Kain trots beside her, horn slashing any that attempt to attack.

Tired of being left alone, I glide toward the pair and grab my sword from the belt at my hip. As soon as my feet hit the ground, I step to Zelle's left flank position. She's light on her feet, and more graceful than a ballerina as she attacks the next trio. I slash at the knees and she stabs their necks. Kain makes a high-pitched neigh, kicking another who makes a move to attack, braining him.

"Well, that one won't be useful." Zelle gives the unicorn a look.

"Zelle," I gasp. "I worry how this fight is changing you."

She looks at me with fire in her eyes. "More than this fight has changed me. I am becoming what I was meant to be. Accept this or leave my side."

My heart drops to my stomach and I gulp down a reply. Instead, I turn away from her, a tear falling down my cheek as I take down the nearest Fae soldier. Everything in me wants to stop her, but I don't. I remain at Zelle's side as she slices her way through the small army. She doesn't stop until every single one is bleeding and under her control.

The undead army lay twitching at her feet and she looks down at them with a darkness that makes me want to scream.

Zelle

The bloodlust fuels my moves, I'm not sure if it's me or the dagger, but I don't mind the killing at all. I finally feel truly free. The blade is light in my hand as one by one the Fae fell at my feet with each arc of my blade.

Dark blood covers the ground but the Fae themselves rise, no longer what they once were. The small army has transformed. Cavill steps forward as my men stand behind me. With a slight gesture, he beckons the fledgelings into the cover of the trees. If I am to win against the King, we will have to attack at night, since the sun's rays make my new army smoke.

"They are yours now," Cavill states as he kneels in the darkness.

"I need you all to aid me in the task to take down the King. Together we will end his reign of terror. Once this is done, I will leave this realm to you. I will not keep you under my rule. Cavill will lead you if that is what you want."

With a scary amount of speed, Cavill appears by my side. My guys make a move toward the vampire, but I hold a hand up to stop them. It's not a secret that the guys still don't trust him, but something inside of me tells me that I can.

"We're no longer Fae," Cavill turns and addresses the newlings. "We are what Zelle has named a vampire. Blood is what we crave, that and violence," he smirks. "We have to stay in the shadows when the sun is out or it will burn."

"Why should we do as she asks?" one of the newly changed asks.

I move my mouth to speak but Cavill cuts me off, "Even if you wanted to disobey, her dagger would tame you. But the simple fact is, if you don't—I will have Altair rip you to pieces and feed you to the wolves. Zelle freed us all. Her task is to free those we helped enslave. We must reconcile what atrocities the King had us commit."

Then something magical happens. Each of my new vampires kneel. They first bow to me and then to Cavill.

"Will dusk work for you guys? That will give us all time to rest and let the sun mostly set," I question.

"Yes, my Queen, midday we can move back toward the castle. There are enough trees between here and there to keep us under their cover," Cavill replies.

Curling my lips, I squeeze the dagger. "Queen? I am not your queen. I killed that bitch of a queen, I am your savior."

A hush falls over the group, but Cavill takes my venom with grace. He bows lightly. "My apologies."

"Accepted. My men and I will return to our camp.

Will you be near if we need help?" I ask, more out of courtesy. I know that I can order them, but that would make me just like the Fae Queen. The dagger and magic have changed me, but that doesn't mean that I will be cruel without reason.

"As you wish, our Savior," Cavill and Altair state at the same time.

I nod to them before I take Xavier's hand and lead him back toward camp. We walk a little way before I glance at him. In the heat of battle, he questioned me and I was a little rough with him. I didn't mean it that way, but I'm not the shy woman I once was.

"Are you upset with me?" I question, walking a little faster.

"No. Maybe. I'm not sure," my beautiful angel replies without looking at me.

"I will not apologize for my actions today. We have a task at hand and I'll do what must be done to achieve it," I speak as much for myself as for him.

"Even if it means acting as those that you mean to free this land from?" Xavier questions.

"I'm nothing like them," I counter.

"For a moment in that battle, I no longer knew who you were. That is why I asked you to leave with me, but you refused," he snaps.

"I was fighting for our lives," I retort. Xavier stops walking.

"That may be, but there is no reason for you to be cruel," he turns toward me with a frown. "I didn't leave you then, but if you continue to go down this dark path, I will have no choice."

"If that is how you feel, so be it. But for the first time in my life, I'm no longer a slave and I'm still figuring out who I am. It might be a bumpy path but I will find my way. The one thing I do know is you four are meant to be with me. Of that, I am certain," I fight back tears. His face doesn't change. Biting my lip, I drop his hand and walk toward the others.

"What was that about?" Wren asks, raising a brow at me.

"Nothing, just a little chat between Xavier and I," I tell him, not wanting to air my personal laundry with the group. Some things should be kept private. Especially when one of my lovers doubts me.

Thankfully, Wren doesn't ask again, so we trek in awkward silence to our sleeping bags in the clearing.

"Xavier, you and Wren need to sleep. You two let us rest too long," I say with a yawn.

"I don't require sleep," Xavier says as he disappears into the trees that surround us.

"But I do," Wren answers. He curls up on the makeshift bed patting the spot next to him as he looks up at me. "Join me?"

"I will soon," I promise but my mind is reeling with the thought that we need to go over the plan before I can rest.

I look over to see Wren smile. No sooner do his lips straighten than his eyes close and he drifts off.

"You two want to sleep as well?" I turn to Flynn and Kain who have been very quiet.

"I can use some rest." Kain stretches his hands over

169

his head. "All the shifting and fighting have worn on me."

I'm glad that he can admit his fatigue to me. I move toward him and kiss his cheek before wrapping my hair around him and humming softly. He lays back on his mat, a dreamy look in his eyes. "Rest," I whisper.

As I stand, Flynn steps to my side. He and I move away toward the firepit. Flynn quickly begins building a fire while I take a seat on the farther log.

"Maybe I should get some kindling," Flynn suggests, shrugging his shoulders.

As if on cue, Xavier comes forward with an arm full of twigs and dumps them on the ground.

"Thank you," I say, but don't look up to see if Xavier hears me.

The angel does something that surprises me and takes a seat next to me. He extends his wing around me and pulls me in close. The tension I was holding eases and I lean into his side.

"I want to be with you, but understand that I only question you because I care. Not to undermine you or anything of that nature. We have to go into this fight together, if we don't we will surely lose," Xavier whispers.

My face heats. I know I shouldn't be angry, I can see the wisdom in Xavier's words, but I can't stop the feeling. This small stretch of time has been the only time in my life I felt I was in control and to have someone question my motives burns me to my core. Still, as I look at Xavier, my budding love for him tampers the heat enough to bear.

"I need you. We belong together, of that much I am sure." I hesitate as my throat tightens. "But I will not back down on ridding the realm of the King, no matter how much darkness I must take on. It won't last forever." I dare to look into the angel's eyes.

Xavier flinches at my gaze. The wing that is draped along my back shivers, the feathers tickling my neck. Deep down, I know he's right, the power I hold is bound to change me. The question is, will it be worth it?

"Can you love me despite the power I must wield to free us?" I inch my lips a breath apart from his.

There's a moment of tension. Xavier's eyes flash golden and a tear falls from my right eye. I almost turn away, but before I can his lips meet mine with a fire I have yet to experience in my lifetime. Heat rushes through my body. Xavier grips the back of my neck as his lips pry mine open, his hot tongue lapping into my mouth. The cocoon of his soft wings pressing against me is such a stark contrast, I think I might expire.

Xavier ends the kiss. Holding my chin, his eyes bore into me leaving me feeling naked as the day I was born. Something about the moment makes me feel stripped down to my soul.

"I will stand by you, however hard it may be for me to watch. Only promise me you'll leave this guise behind when you are free," he breathes. "Your soul is too beautiful to hold this taint."

Holding back a full blown sob, I nod. Even though I've only known these males for a short time, I can't imagine my life without a single one of them.

Xavier's lips soften from the firm line of worry and he pulls me in for a hug. As soon as my face nestles into the crook of his neck, I lose it. Every sadness I've held inside comes out in a flood of tears. Even if I wanted to, I wouldn't be able to stop the heaving of my chest. Xavier tightens his arms, comforting me without words, and I sink into his hold to allow myself to let it all out. In the end, the tears dry up and I'm left feeling exhausted.

"Thank you for trusting me with that." Xavier kisses my tear-stained cheek and opens his wings. A cool breeze washes over me, drying my face and clearing my head. "Now, come. You must rest," Xavier commands.

We tiptoe through the campsite until we approach Kain's resting form. Flynn is snoring on the other side of the fire. Xavier tucks me into Kain's side, drops a kiss on my head and covers us with a blanket. I have half a mind to thank him, but Kain's arm wraps around me and my eyes close without another thought.

Zelle

I don't know how long I slept, only that when Kain nudges me awake, I feel lost in time. My brain won't restart for a moment. All I can do is lay there staring into his hazel eyes in wonder.

"Zelle, it's time to go," Kain's voice is tender, but his expression is worrisome.

"What's happening?" I ask as I stand with his help.

"Seems the King, himself, has decided to come and face us. We need to regroup and figure out what we plan to do," he tells me.

With the sun still up, our army will not be able to help and dread fills me. I was sure that we would be able to free the Fae from this menace but my plan hinges on being able to use the vampires. I should know better than to count on things before they happen, but I was sure that we would win.

"Where are the others?" I ask my fallen angel.

"Warning the creatures, they should be able to help from under the cover of the trees," he reassures me.

Why am I freaking out now? We were going to the palace to confront the King. At least the other plan was

ROWAN THALIA & JENÉE ROBINSON

on my terms. We can't let this detour us. On the bright side, I'll have the pleasure of killing Thayer today.

Xavier and I move into the cover of the trees and it's not long before I notice figures lounging under the shade of them. It's a little unsettling how they can sit so motionless. We find Flynn, Kain, and Wren chatting with Altair and Cavill and relief fills me when I see we are all safe.

Kain moves so that Xavier and I can join the little circle.

"My Lady," Cavill says with a little bow.

"There is no need for that," I tell him. "I am only in charge until we defeat the King. I have no intention of keeping you all enslaved. I may be your creator but once we liberate the Fae, the same is your fate. If my men are willing, I want to return to the mortal realm and find my true parents," I promise.

Cavill and Altair just give me a little nod in understanding.

"How will you be able to aid us with the upcoming fight?" I ask.

"If we can lure them into the shadows, we can win. The sun is too high in the sky still for us to fight in the open. Once it starts setting we can step out of the shade but not sooner," Altair states.

"I am sorry that I doomed you to the dark," I say, lowering my head.

Cavill takes a step towards me, raising my chin with a gentle hand. "We may not be free in the daylight hours, but we rule the night. You did what no one else could, you freed us from that wretched Queen. It has been an adjustment but I have no ill will toward you."

I look from him to the other vampires and they all nod in agreement.

"Now that that is out of the way, we have to plan how to get the King and his men into the trees," Flynn says, flashing his signature smile at me.

"I don't think that your smolder will work on them," I comment with a smile.

"I mean, it could," he counters.

"There will be time for you to flirt later," Kain tells us, "we have an army approaching."

"Yes, I know. Wren and I are the ones they will target. Maybe we could be bait."

My men shift uncomfortably on their heels.

Wren is the first to speak, "I don't think that's a good idea. The Fae are fast on their feet, I don't think that you will be able to outrun them."

"Well, I only need to beat them into the trees. Once there I can use my dagger to change them or my vampires will take them down," I retort. "If we wait for them to get to the tree row, they will think that they can outrun me. Not knowing what I have in store for them."

"I think we all should be bait." Kain says, moving toward me until he has a hand wrapped around my waist. "They have to know that all of us escaped together and may be suspicious that we are hidden in the trees. If that happens, then I don't think that they will follow you into the trees."

175

"You are always the voice of reason aren't you?" I ask as I smile up at him.

"I don't think I'd go that far," he replies as he places a kiss on my forehead.

"So, the five of us will act as if we are camping there and pretend that we don't realize that the army is coming. Once we see them, we will head into the trees and start the fighting. You all are free to kill any of the Fae, but leave the King to me. Does he have any elemental powers I should be aware of?" I question.

Wren and Altair glance at each other, before Altair speaks up, "Water, definitely. He doesn't have fire. The one reason he married the Queen was to keep the Fire Fae in check. I'm not sure if he has any others."

"I can confirm water, but he wasn't blessed with much power at all. He is the last of a dying line. It was foretold that his heir would possess the most magic a single Fae was gifted in centuries, that is why the Queen was so hellbent on a baby. It wasn't a maternal thing, she was greedy," Cavill adds.

"That sounds like another reason to end the King's life," Wren comments.

"You better get your camp set up. They are less than a mile from where we are now," Cavill breaks in. "That gives us less than half an hour."

"How do you know that?" I ask.

"It's another gift that came with the transformation," Cavill states, "our ears are more sensitive now."

"What else changed?" I question, my curiosity getting the better of me.

"Speed and strength, that's all I know for sure, there

hasn't been much time to test our limits. Once we are free, that will be the time for us to explore," he answers.

"Soon," I promise. Kain and I turn with our hands linked and we follow the others into the clearing.

"Are you ready for this?" he asks.

"I am. There is something in me, telling me that I am meant to end the King's reign. I've never been more sure of anything, besides you four in my life," I answer honestly.

"Please stay close to one of us," Kain raises a hand. "Before you protest, I know you can handle yourself. It's more for our peace of mind than yours." Kain smiles lightly.

It's odd to think that a few short days ago I thought no one in the world cared about me. Looking into Kain's eyes, there's no way I can deny his request. "I shall do my best to comply," I say with a small curtsy.

The hairs on my arms begin to rise as a tension rolls through my small army. This is it. We are preparing for battle. As much as I try to remain calm, sweat breaks out along my forehead. Regardless of the Goddess' gifts, I feel small and unready for what I know is to come even though it also feels right.

"If anyone has an ailment that needs healing, now is the time to ask," I shout absently. Of course, the vampires have no need of my hair, but my men may.

"We are all in top form," Wren says as he checks over his bow and quiver of arrows. "You should hydrate and find a spot where you can slip in and out of the fray with your little stinger." Wren grins as he looks at the dagger at my hip.

I give him my best death glare as I walk over to the water bowl and sip. I know he's right, but I'm used to being the one taking care of others—not the other way around. Kain and Wren share a knowing look and my cheeks flush. So, this is love.

"Indeed, it is love," Xavier swoops in like a mind-reading genius. His white feathers tickle my cheek as he drops a kiss on my forehead. The more I get from these men, the more I want—but now is not the time to think of such things. We need to put our best game faces on and beat Thayer once and for all.

Closing my eyes, I recount every single injury that I had to heal back at the castle. My mind plays a reel of prisoner after prisoner being dragged into my cell. The conditions they were held in—and the ones I wasn't able to heal. A lump forms in my throat and steel hardens my spine. *For them, I must be strong.*

"Keeper of the Dagger," one of the soldiers whispers. "They are near. Quiet, everyone, and get into formation."

A hush falls over the clearing as the soldiers move to obey. Not a soldier myself, I look to Wren. My former guard offers me an elbow before leading me to meet the King's army head on. It's a slight change in plans, but one I'm immediately on board with. I can't wait to see the look on Thayer's face when I don't cower before him.

With my three males protecting me from the rear, Wren and I stride toward the footsteps coming from the King's army. They finally come into sight when we crest a small hill. The sun ricochets off the Fae vambraces and helmets making me squint as I try to place Thayer among them.

"King Thayer!" I shout, stepping out into the open. "I wish to parley."

A belly laugh answers me as the Fae part for their ruler. Thayer steps forward, his eyes twinkling. "What could you possibly have to say to me that I'd care to hear, Princess?"

Unperturbed, I look him in the eye before closing the distance between us. Perhaps he, too, will underestimate me and this fight will be swift. "I wish for my freedom, and those of my men. If you grant it, we will leave with no more ill will," I lie through an overly sweet smile.

"And what would I gain from letting you go? You've already taken a number of my soldiers, not to mention my Queen," Thayer growls. His hand moves more swiftly than I can account for and suddenly, he has a grip of my hair, pulling me to my knees. Refusing to utter even a peep, I glare up at him.

The King spits in my face and then looks up. "And you, Wren, one of my most trusted guards. Have you forsaken your King?"

Wiping my face with one hand, I palm the dagger with the other as I watch a storm roll over my lover's face. "I have not, sire. It is you who have forsaken your people. You who allowed the former Queen to abuse and neglect your subjects. I do not bow to such a King as that," Wren draws his sword. "Unhand the Princess."

My heart is in my throat as I watch them face off. Xavier, Kain, and Flynn tighten their circle behind

Wren. Thick silence clogs the air, only to be squashed by the flap of wings and clop of Kain's hooves. I don't know when Kain shifted, but his horn glows like its aflame.

The grip on my hair loosens, but doesn't leave. Thayer drags me forward, stopping when he's toe to toe with Wren. "You dare!" the King roars, slinging me upward and between them. "For this little piece of ass?" He sneers, licking my face. A thunderous roar fills my ears as the Goddess's power demands restitution. Without thinking, I reach upward to lodge the dagger deep in Thayer's throat. Blood gushes out, covering my face. The change on his skin starts to spread, he seems to be fighting it.

"Run to the trees!" Wren grabs me, pushing me toward Kain as the King's men rush forward.

Zelle

"Is he dead?" I ask in between breaths.

"I'm not sure," Wren replies, still holding on to me.

The vampires are in the shadow of the trees, a look of hunger is in their eyes and a few even lick their lips. If they weren't on my side, I would be a little scared of what they would do to me.

The four of us don't stop until we are in the middle of the vampire army.

"What's the plan now?" Xavier asks.

"We fight. If the Fae want to fight with the King, their death is their choice. I gave him the option to stop all of this and he declined. So be it," I tell him, my tone firm.

"I agree," Wren states as we get a neigh from Kain.

The wait is not long. It's easy to tell when the guards make it to the shade of the trees because that's when the screaming and shrieking begins. I even think I hear a few snarls from the changelings. Our weapons are at the ready when the few that have survived what has waited in the shadows for them emerge. The King's army has determination on their brow and they push on.

"For the King!" the closest one shouts as he runs at me.

In a flash, he is in pieces at my feet. I scan the trees and notice that Cavill is still smoking from leaving his sanctuary of the trees. I nod in thanks as I steady the dagger in my hand as a few more emerge.

"Ready?" I question my men.

"Aye," Wren and Xavier say in unison. No neigh from Kain, but he stomps a hoof in answer.

"Cavill, you and the others are to stay under shade until it is safe for you otherwise," I order, my voice not wavering.

"As you wish," he says with a grunt.

"Why did you do that?" Xavier asks, his brow furrowing.

"I have already taken their lives once and then asked them to fight for me, there is no need to harm them more if it's unnecessary," I tell him, before adding, "please don't question my decisions again."

He gives me a little bow and we stand firm as the guards try to attack. The closest one gets gored with Kain's horn as he is thrown over him at the same time. He lands with a thud and from this angle he was dead before he hit the ground.

The next one is met with Wren's sword. He is parrying a blow when another Fae joins the fight and he doesn't skip a beat at fending off both. The clink of metal seems to ring in my ears as I watch one of my men fight just because he loves me. Not only that, I am right about his once King. Wren spins on his heel as he cuts one of the Fae down and arcs his blade through the other one. They both fall lifeless at his feet.

The sight of Wren covered in blood turns me on but I tell myself that now is not the time to jump him. *Down, girl, there will be time for that later.*

Xavier isn't to be outdone, he blows back the Fae that ran at him with a gust from his wings. It makes the Fae stumble and drop his sword, just as Xavier expects. He flies toward the man and punches him in the face. The blow causes his head to fling back in one movement. The crack of his neck sends shivers down my spine, in a delicious way as I wait for my turn to join in the carnage.

The first one to get near me, swings his sword lazily, as if he isn't even trying. I, on the other hand, strike with precision, slicing his neck open wide. His sword clatters to the ground as he wraps his hands to cover the cut. He falls to his knees before me for a few seconds before he tumbles to the ground to change.

Paying him no more mind, I attack the next one. Once my blade has scored him, he transforms faster than the one still withering at my feet. My new minion bows before me.

"How may I serve you, my Queen?" he mutters, looking at the ground.

I pull his chin up, "You are free. If you wish to repay me, fight to keep your freedom."

"I shall," he swears as he reaches for his fallen sword.

"Thank you," I state as I watch him run toward the oncoming Fae.

My men haven't moved too far from where they started their fight. Two that made it past my guys run straight for me. A quick learner, I sidestep and spin with my blade out at the same time, slicing them both. The flayed Fae grab at their guts, but my blade has already poisoned them.

"Zelle!" the King yells as he lumbers out of the trees, blood staining his clothes.

A smile tips my lips, "Finally. It took you long enough."

The wounded royal doesn't reply, only grunts and continues forward. My eyes notice a movement and I turn to see Kain move towards him, his horn down as if he is going to attack.

I call out to him, "One hit."

If anyone besides me wanted revenge from what the King had done it would be my shifter. Every injury I healed him from came from either the Queen or King. Both had it out for my unicorn. My heart aches as the memories flash before me. Allowing the kill to be his, I watch as Kain rises on his back hooves. In a flash of movement, he slams his front hooves against King Thayer's chest. I'd thought he would gore him with his horn, but he only tramples the King before moving on to the next Fae.

The King doesn't stay down long. Once he rises, he sets his sights on me. The wicked smile that turns up his lips gives me a shiver. He steps closer, his hands flickering at his sides as he starts to summon water. Thayer tries to aim a stream at me, but it falls short.

I can't stop the laugh that escapes my lips, "It's no wonder you haven't any children."

"Why you little slut. How dare you speak to me that way," Thayer says as he stalks closer. He picks up one of the fallen's blades and raises it at me. "Do you really think that little dagger of yours can kill me?"

I nod a yes. I'm not going to get caught up in words and lose focus.

"Then give me your best shot," he taunts, a sneer on his lips.

"Nah, I think it's better you come to me," I say unfazed but mentally slapping myself for talking back.

Thayer increases his speed and begins waving the sword around like an idiot. Does he even know how to use it? It's almost comical to watch his movements, erratic as they are, but there is a rhythm to them. It's amazing that I found a pattern to them at all. But with a little focus, I know that I can hit his heart with one blow if I time my hit with when he will let his arm down.

Thayer continues his approach. Biding my time, I wait until the perfect time to strike. Without hesitation, I take it. My dagger hits its mark sinking deep into his heart. Before pulling it out, I twist the blade. Blood drips to the ground from the dagger's tip and Thayer falls to the grass, clutching his chest.

As if a gong has been rung, the fighting stops. I stand frozen with the dagger in hand scanning the fray, all eyes are on me. One by one my men rush to my side.

Wren lowers my hand and places a kiss on my forehead before kneeling down and taking the King by the hair as he severs the head from his body with one swift cut of his blade.

"That will do it," Wren comments, looking over his shoulder at me with a smile.

Wren offers the head to me. I take it in my free hand, turn to the onlookers and raise both hands into the air. "King Thayer is dead. His rule is over. No more shall any living thing be tortured by his hand. I order the dungeons to be emptied and all Fae in this realm to be free."

One by one the crowd drops to one knee. "All hail the Queen!" a voice calls out.

The breath leaves my body as the chant grows louder and louder as more voices join. Aghast, I look to Wren who falls to one knee and joins the chant. I cannot be ... Queen!

"Please," I call out. "I am not fit to wear a crown!"

"Ah, but you are," Xavier takes the head from my hand and tosses it to Flynn. "And this realm needs someone like you to lead them out of the darkness."

"But," I stare with my mouth agape. "I have a family to find."

"Yes, but that is neither here nor there, Blondie. As ruler, you would be free to travel as much as you please," Flynn adds with his signature grin.

"Aye, you are exactly what this realm needs," Kain shifts so suddenly I blink.

"Besides, here you can wed us all," Wren whispers in my ear and my face heats.

A tide of emotions washed over me. Could I actually become Queen of Wolgast? It is a heavy responsibility to take on, especially since I was once enslaved here. The more I think about it, the more the idea appeals to me. How else would I ensure that the next ruler doesn't follow Thayer's path? With that, my decision is sealed.

"I accept," I give my best curtsy to the crowd of Fae and a shout of glee rolls through the crowd.

"I guess we should march back to the castle then," Wren smirks, offering me an elbow.

"Our Queen will not walk," Kain snorts as he shifts.

Xavier laughs. He and Wren help me onto Kain's back and then flank my sides as Kain carries me to the front of the line of soldiers. Flynn tosses up a flask before whistling for the troops to follow as we begin the trip back to Wolgast.

"If you would allow," Cavill runs up to our side. "My team can travel faster than even Fae now that the sun is setting. We would like to go ahead of you and announce your arrival. It would be our honor to weed out any naysayers before you arrive."

My heart swells at the forethought of the soldier and I nod. "Let it be done. Do not harm any who would submit to my reign. And please, begin the release of the prisoners. I'd like all of my subjects to remain of their own free will."

"Yes, your Majesty," Cavill bows before he disappears into the shadows.

"Will you still release them from your will?" Wren places a hand on my ankle.

"If they choose it," I answer truthfully even though the thought saddens me.

A great sorrow shadows my heart as we march on. Try as I might, I can't pinpoint why my eyes keep filling with tears. With nothing but the sound of boots and hooves crunching against the earth, I'm left to my thoughts.

Memory after memory of my enslavement bombard me. The closer we get to the castle, the heavier the sorrow. In my tears, I realize I'll have my work cut out for me to erase the evil taint from this place.

"And yet, you will do it," Xavier grabs my hand and kisses it.

"Reading my mind?" I sniffle.

"Only when you project louder than a volcano erupting, my love," Xavier says with a golden flash to his eyes.

Flynn

Approaching the gates of Wolgast without chains binding me is a weird feeling. Stranger still is the awe written in the faces that line up to watch our procession. If anyone would have asked me if I'd be a Queen's consort days ago, I'd have laughed in their face. In hours, I'll be just that. My thieving little heart still hasn't processed it all.

"All hail the Queen!" The chant reverberates through the crowd as we weave down the path toward the castle.

Zelle was insistent we arrive at night so that her full army could show its face. She's told the vampires on several occasions they are free of her, but they will not leave her side. I can't blame them really, I never want to, either.

It's all been a wild ride. To think I came here in order to find Zelle and get a reward for returning her to her parents. In no part of my imagination did I foresee falling in love with her and sharing her with not only three other men, but an entire realm.

The question nagging at me is whether I can live up

to these expectations. I've always lived my own life, free of the rules and constraints that many others place upon themselves. I've begged, borrowed, and stolen more times than I can count. Does a moth ever resist the flame? I guess we will find out.

"Stop daydreaming, you're falling behind!" Xavier hisses from his station next to Zelle's left leg. Easy for him to say, he isn't sniffing a unicorn tail as we walk. As if he knows my thoughts, Kain swishes his tail, hitting me in the face.

Making a face at Xavier, I quicken my pace so that I'm elbow to wing with the angel. At least by his side, I won't face the indignity of huffing rainbow farts. Xavier looks over to me with a wry grin before lightly flapping his wings. It's just enough to tickle my cheek with his feathers and raise my ire.

"Why must you two be so annoying?" I growl.

Kain chuffs and Xavier laughs, neither are helping. The only thing that cools me is the small laugh that escapes Zelle's lips, like the tinkling of a bell. She and I make eye contact and my heart thumps against my ribs. I need my first kiss with her. It's an ache that's festered these long nights since we became a partnership.

"Be patient," Zelle mouths with a smile.

There's part of me that wants to rip her from her seat and kiss her silly, but, of course, I won't. I want her to come to me. If the stars are kind, it will happen this night.

"You realize she's got a lot on her plate just now, correct?" Xavier nudges me.

My cheeks flush with embarrassment over my selfishness. "Yes, of course," I fake nonchalantly.

We finally approach the steps to the castle. Zelle slides off of Kain's back and turns to the throng of subjects who have followed. Her face is perfectly framed by the moonlight, her long hair grown back over the last days flows around her like a cape hiding her blood-spattered clothing.

"Residents of Wolgast," Zelle's voice cuts through the air like a knife. "King Thayer is no more. By my hand his life was ended and I would ask for your blessing to assume the throne. If there is anyone who rejects me as Queen, let them step forward now."

A whisper rolls though the audience, but none step forward. Instead, one by one every soul falls to one knee in reverence. A hush falls over the courtyard and a tear falls from Zelle's eye. Cavill and Wren share a look before the vampire soldier steps back and opens the door to the castle.

"From this night, let it be known that Wolgast is ruled by Queen Zelle and her four consorts Wren, Kain, Xavier, and Flynn!" Cavill drops the bottom of his spear to the marble three times. "Please honor them with three cheers." The crowd goes wild and I step to Zelle's side. Without my noticing, Kain shifted to his manly form and is draped in a soldier's cloak. He and I stand shoulder to shoulder, pride bursting in my heart.

Zelle

Stepping into a bath after such an ordeal almost knocks me out. My muscles immediately relax as Flynn washes the dried blood from my body ever so gently. It occurs to me that I don't know where my other men are, but then flickers of memory pass and I remember that they're downstairs tending to the details of my coronation. I only half-heard the conversation as I was being led away by Flynn.

With any luck, they will all head this way before Flynn and I make it to the bed. I don't have very much sexual experience, but I'm keen to have them all next to me this night.

"Are you falling asleep on me?" Flynn lets out a small laugh as he lathers my hair. I hate how quickly it grew back. I'm starting to wonder if it's worth keeping the magic. It would be so freeing not to have the weight of it surrounding me. Realizing I can also cut it with the dagger anytime, I jump out of the bath, almost slipping.

"Where are you going?

"To get the dagger! I want you to cut my hair short!"

I yell over my shoulder as I sprint into the next room. As I come around the wall, I run smack into a wall of muscle.

"Well, that's quite a greeting," Kain chuckles as he steadies me by holding my arms.

Wrinkling my nose, I giggle. "I need the dagger so you can cut this damn hair."

Kain's mouth spreads into a wide smile and he releases me. Leaving me standing naked, he turns and rummages through the pile of dirty clothing until he finds the weapon. "Got it!" He raises his hand above his head. "Off with her HAIR!" he jokes as he saunters over to me.

"Indeed, maybe you should cut it off on the balcony, I don't want the hair all over the floor," I bite my lip as I move toward the veranda.

"As you wish. Lean your head over the railing and I'll make quick work of it. How short?" Kain asks as he runs the blade over the leg of his pants.

"To my shoulders," I state as I lean my head over and drop the locks to the ground below.

Kain is swift and precise as he cuts. The strands fall to the ground with a light puff. When I straighten, it feels as if the weight of the world has lifted. "How does it look? Is it still blonde?" I ask nervously. If the magic is gone, the locks will be brown.

"You look stunning. And yes, still golden as the rays of the sun, love."

"Oh good. The prisoners may yet need my gift. By the time we wake in the morning it should be long enough again for me to use the incantation," I smile.

"Come to the bath with us!" I grab Kain's hand and drag him to the bathroom. "Where is everyone else?"

Kain laughs. "Slow down, my Queen. Wren and Xavier send word that they will be up to tuck you in within the hour. There was a security breach and they've set off to handle it. I came up to make sure you were also protected. Before you ask, I don't have any other information. Let's get you back in the bath, you're shivering."

Frowning, I allow him to lead me back to Flynn who's laid back against the tub with his eyes closed. "Honey, I'm home!" I yell, startling him.

"I was beginning to wonder if you'd stolen her away again." Flynn grins. "Come back in here, you beautiful Goddess!"

Kain gives me the sweetest smile before dragging me into the water. It takes a little maneuvering but we settle with Flynn at the rear, me between his legs, and Kain between mine. The water flows around us in a bubbly warmth that zaps the stress of war from my bones in minutes. The ease in which we lay together is surprising, but it makes me happy to know that these two can be polite.

"If we don't move to the bed, I'm going to fall asleep between the two of you and drown," I chirp.

"To bed!" Flynn cheers with a fist in the air.

Kain stands, stepping out of the tub with the grace of his unicorn. I can't help but stare at every defined edge of his muscles. I've touched almost every inch of him, but I've never before had this view and I quite like it.

"Like what you see?" He blows a kiss before wrapping a towel about his waist.

Blinking, I nod. Kain chuckles as he reaches for my hand to help me out of the bath. Within moments, the two men are patting me with towels and planting kisses along my curves. Every thought of sleep flies out of the window as my body heats under their ministrations.

"Take me to bed or lose me forever," I gasp as Kain's hand caresses the swell of my breast.

"We will take you to bed, but there will be no sex, sweet Zelle. You must be fresh for your coronation in a few short hours. Once you have the crown, we will consummate this new relationship with all of your consorts present. I am under strict orders from Wren," Kain whispers in my ear.

"That doesn't mean we can't give her a massage before she rests," Flynn says wickedly as he covers my mouth with his. This is deep and consuming. I whimper as he pulls away, needing more.

The two men share a look before Kain lifts me in his arms and walks me to the bed. He lays me down gently, then turns me on my belly and begins rubbing my back while Flynn rubs my feet. I squirm for a moment, pouting. But within moments, I find my eyes are too heavy to keep open and I drift off.

※

There is a pounding with urgency on my door, rousing me from my sleep. Kain and Flynn sit upright at the same time.

"Yes?" I question from the bed as both guys scramble to find some clothes.

A muffled voice comes from behind the door, "Sorry to bother you, my Queen. We have your dress for the coronation. There is little time to dress you and get you ready."

"Give me a moment," I call as Flynn throws under-things at me. The servants may help me into the clothing but that doesn't mean they have to see all of me. I pull them on in a flash and nod to Kain as he is already at the door after dressing.

"Sorry again," the first maid says as she moves toward the bed. She is carrying purple jewels and a matching gown is brought in by two others.

"Where…where did you find this?" I ask, stumbling over my words a little. "It's all breathtaking."

"Your new Fae, the pale ones. They worked with lightning speed and created this all for you," one of them says, a little bit of disgust in her tone. I'm sure she thought that I missed that part, because she pulls her lips into a smile.

I do not return false warmth. "If you have a distaste for my new Fae, you are free to leave. I will not force anyone to serve me if they don't want to. This kingdom will no longer be run on fear, I am not a cruel ruler. But I will not have anyone speak ill of the vampires. They have been at my side with no question of loyalty.

As you have free will, so do they and they choose to stay with me." I grit my teeth as I move closer to her.

"I'm s-sorry, my Queen," she stutters. "I will provide superior service and not speak badly about any Fae, vampire or not. I didn't mean for my words to come out that way."

I clasp her on the shoulder and say honestly, "Thank you, that is all I ask."

"What about us?" Flynn asks."There's no way I can put these dirty rags back on," he grimaces at the dirty pile of clothes he left on the floor.

On cue, Jarica enters my chambers with piles of purple fabric and a smirk on her lips. "You didn't think that we would leave out our Queen's consorts."

Xavier and Wren enter the room mere moments after the vampire. I breathe a sigh of relief to have all my guys under one roof once again.

"Where have you two been?" I ask moving around the maids to embrace my loves.

"Here and there," Wren says, not giving me a straight answer.

I raise my brow at him.

"I promise, nothing that you need worry about now. Let these ladies get you ready, the people are waiting for their new Queen." He presses a kiss to my lips.

"I will drop it for now, but I want to know," I promise him, before turning back to the maids. "I'm ready, where do we begin?"

The three approach me and start to dress me, pulling the fabric down over my head and tightening and straightening until they are happy. They pull me to the mirror and I gasp as I take in my reflection. Is that really me? Aside from needing my hair tamed, my newly cut locks are a little unruly, I do look like a ruler. The beautiful A-Line ballgown is strapless with a sweetheart neckline. The purple fabric is the most comfortable I've ever worn. It's not itchy like the ones I'm used to.

"If you move to the vanity, I can fix your hair, that way the crown will sit on top and stay," one of the ladies says.

Moving toward the vanity, I glance back at my guys. They are struggling a little to get into their new duds and I can swear that Jarica is in the shadows laughing at them. With silent gestures, I direct the other two maids to aid the guys while I sit to have my hair fixed.

As I sit, the maid begins to speak, "It's a shame you cut your hair. It was so gorgeous."

"It grows very fast, I didn't want it weighing me down for the coronation," I explain.

"My queen, you have nothing to explain to me. I am just a little jealous that you have such amazing hair. When I was younger, a virus swept our little village and robbed me of mine," she tells me as she lowers her hood just a little to show a bald spot where her hair should be.

"Oh, I'm so sorry. I have some healing powers. If you would like, once my locks grow out a little I can see if I can heal that for you. I can't promise that it will work but I'm willing to try," I say with a small smile.

"If you have time once you are crowned, I would be grateful for such kindness," she says shyly.

"Jarica," I call as the maid begins placing the crown onto my head.

"Yes, m'lady?" the vampire asks a moment later.

"This Fae here, what's your name, dear?" I ask.

"Alette, my Queen." the shy maid replies in a small voice.

"I want you to make sure that I remember to try and heal this Fae. Can you do that for me? I fear once I start all the new tasks of ruling that I will forget, I don't want that to happen," I comment.

"I will not forget," the vampire promises.

It doesn't take Alette long to prepare my hair as it is so short. She brushes the unruly locks and weaves small white flowers into either side.Then she adds a little makeup to dress me up before adding jewels. I'm pleased that she picked a golden necklace with four amethyst stones, earrings to match, and also a ring.

"The vampires wanted you to have a stone on your necklace and ring for each of your men. I hope they didn't overstep," Jarica explains.

"Not at all, this is more than I deserve," I say, holding back tears.

In the mirror I watch as Wren walks up and clasps Jarica on the shoulder. "No, you deserve the world," he beams as our eyes meet in the reflection. Jarica nods in agreement.

"We all do," I say as I stand and hook an arm into Wren's.

We thank the maids for their aid, they nod and scurry off to dress themselves now. I have a smile plastered on my face. How did my life go from a living hell to this?

"It was your destiny," Xavier states as he takes my other arm.

"We are going to have to have a chat about your little mind-reading ability later," I tell him.

He just shrugs as Kain and Flynn lead the way to the coronation.

Zelle

Taking up a position between my four handsome males, I nod to Jarica that we are ready to proceed. The striking vampire taps her spear on the floor three times. The door to my suite opens and Altair and Cavill appear decked out in the finest of Fae armor.

"Your subjects await in the courtyard," Altair takes a bow.

"Lead on," Wren answers.

With the sweep of his cape, Altair acquiesces. He, Cavill, and Jarica lead us back down the stairs and through the castle. The gleaming gold walls and shining floor seem to shine with a new vigor as we walk through the great hall. It isn't lost on me that the old throne room has been emptied of the old ruler's throne. My heart swells. Reaching for Wren's hand, I give it a squeeze. He smiles and we proceed out the side entrance to the gardens.

When we step out onto the terrace, I'm left breathless. The courtyard has been transformed into a wonderland of faery lights and bright-pink roses. All of the kingdom is seated in half circles that surround a large flower-covered throne.

"It's so beautiful," I gasp.

"I'm glad you are pleased," Xavier winks. "I had to fly pretty far to gather the perfect flowers. I wanted this to be special."

Tears fill my eyes as I look from Xaiver to Wren. So, this is what they've been up to all evening. "Thank you."

"It is time," the court priest smiles before inclining his head toward me. He guides me to stand in front of the throne. Xavier and Wren kneel on my right while Flynn and Kain kneel at my left side.

"Subjects of Wolgast. We gather this night to welcome our new queen," he opens his palms to the crowd before turning to me "Will you swear to use your power for good. To uphold the Law and provide merciful justice, in all of your judgements?"

"I will," I answer with a lump in my throat.

"Do you always swear to consult your counsel upon Fae law and return the land of Alba to the true ways of the Fae?"

"I will."

"It is with a full heart that I solemnly swear to rule Wolgast fairly and justly. I hold each soul here in my heart as I would my own children, had I any. My subjects will have mercy and love until I no longer rule," I speak from the heart.

The priest touches his heart before picking up the crown resting on a pillow beside him. "It is with honor

I place this upon your head and dub thee Queen of Wolgast," he says with a booming voice.

The crowd cheers as I step forward. "May I present my consorts," I point to each male as I call their name and they stand.

"Please know that your health and safety are our priority. If any need assistance, my throne room will be open to hear your appeals at sunset each evening. Now go and be merry, let us celebrate!" I call out.

It gives me great pleasure to see the smiling faces as they line up to wish me well before dispersing into the garden for food and dancing. A small band of three began to play stringed instruments that I've never seen. The ambiance is one I've yet to witness in my entire life. Every soul seems to be happy and relaxed, even the soldiers standing guard at the perimeter of the dais of my throne.

"You've done well." Xavier steps to my side. His face is near unreadable but his voice is laced with honey.

"I'm glad you approve." I laugh. A servant walks up with a tray full of Feywine-filled flutes and I grab two, handing one to Xavier. We clink glasses before taking a sip. The bubbly drink tickles my nose but goes down smoothly after that.

"How did you and Wren manage to put all of this together in so short a time?" I look around to see my other three consorts chatting with Altair and Cavill.

"Ah, that is a secret, my love. You will soon come to realize that we will move heaven and earth to make your days happier," Xavier whispers before placing a kiss on my forehead.

I accept the secret, for now. Though I'm not sure I will ever get used to them doing things for me. My life has never been one where my needs were ever considered. *Who knew a magical dagger would change so much.*

As I finish my thought, my breath halts. I realize I don't remember where I set the dagger last. Patting my side on instinct, I begin to panic.

"Shh," Wren steps to my side. "The dagger is here," he lifts his cloak to show me the weapon strapped neatly to his belt. "It doesn't really go with your outfit, but I figured you would want it near."

"Thank you, Wren. I think you should be the guardian of the dagger for now. Until I figure out what to do with it next," I state as I place a hand at his elbow.

"As you wish, my Queen."

Before I can say anything more, Flynn and Kain join us. "How long before it's socially acceptable for us to slip out of here?" Flynn asks. The heat in his eyes could burn down a building.

"I haven't the faintest idea." I shrug. "As a lifelong prisoner, I've never been to a party."

Flynn's eyes widen and he folds his body into a low bow. "Forgive me. I'd all but forgotten. This is your night and your first party. We should live it to the fullest. May I have your first dance?"

A lightness passes between us as I take my consort's hand. Flynn leads me to the center of the dancefloor and spins me in a neat circle. I've never danced before, but Flynn is a good leader and after the first few steps, we fall into a rhythm. Couples join us one by one and my heart fills with joy.

"Is this everything you could've dreamed up?" Flynn asks with a smug smile.

"So much more. I thought the tower was the highlight of my life as a prisoner. There was never a time I thought I would be free, let alone rule the kingdom that once held me captive," I reply, honestly.

"What if I told you that I wasn't here by mistake?" he asks a little cautiously.

"I'm not sure I understand," I answer, my brows pinched.

"I was sent by your parents," he whispers as we sway to the music.

My heart stops at his words.

"W...why did you wait until now to tell me?" I question, but don't pull away.

"I started so many times, but then I fell for you. Before I could get you alone, we had to escape prison and battle the King and his army. There didn't seem like an appropriate time to just casually drop the bomb. No way was I going to be like, 'by the way, your long lost parents had me searching for you.' You may have started out as my mission but you are more than that to me now. Please understand why I waited and don't be upset with me," he explains with a croak in his voice.

I pull him closer to me, hugging his body to mine, "When can I meet them?"

"Whenever you are ready, I know you have a lot on your plate now that you rule this kingdom. I could travel to the human realm and return with them. Would that be to your satisfaction?" he asks, still holding me tight.

"Yes," I whisper, pulling back so I can look him in the eyes.

"Oh no, please don't cry, my Queen," he says, wiping a tear from my cheek.

"I promise, these are tears of joy. I have everything I could have ever wanted and more. This is the best day ever," I tell him.

"Technically, it's night," he counters, "but I think we will be on vampire hours from here on out so, day it is."

I press my lips to his to stop him from talking, and just live in this moment. When we break apart we are both a little breathless.

"Hey, save some of that for me," Kain calls from behind us, moving closer. "Okay if I cut in?"

"I don't mind," I muse but glance at Flynn.

He sighs and says, "Fine. I'm going to have to get used to sharing you anyway."

Kain grins as he takes Flynn's position with his arms wrapped around me. It feels just as wonderful to be in his strong arms as it did Flynn's.

"How did I ever get to be so lucky with you four?" I ask as I lay my head on his shoulder.

"Destiny. You were always meant for us," he replies simply before asking, "why were you crying when you were talking to Flynn?"

"It was a good cry. He was sent by my real parents to find me," I reply.

"And you aren't pissed he is just now telling you?" Kain questions.

"I wanted to be, but honestly, there's no reason. We are free and so are all the people of our territory. Anger has no place in my heart at the moment. It is full of love for the four of you and these people that accepted me as their queen. That is how I plan to rule, so it starts with Flynn," I explain.

"And this is why you will be the favorite ruler of the land," he comments, "When will you meet your parents? Are we heading to the human realm?" Kain asks.

"Let me enjoy being in your arms a little longer and we can go have a chat with the others. It's glorious to just live in this moment right now after all we have survived," I say.

He places a kiss on the back of my hand before saying, "Right you are, my Love."

We sway and move around the dance floor until the band's song finishes.

"I think we need another drink to celebrate you, my Queen," Kain says with a smile.

"Water, this time. That champagne has my head a little fuzzy," I tell him and he laughs.

"Fine, if the Queen wants water, then water she gets."

Kain wraps an arm around my waist and guides me between the other Fae on the dance floor. I love all the smiling faces I see as we pass. In my whole time here, the only Fae that ever smiled were the King and his men. Those bastards, well all but Wren. I hadn't seen a true smile from him until we broke out of the dungeon. We don't stop until we land at the table the other three are at. Kain deposits me in Xavier's lap and heads off in search of water.

"Are you enjoying yourself?" Xavier asks, his hands roaming my body.

"I am. We will have to plan more of these in the months to come; you know, to keep morale up," I answer.

"Well, freeing them from their previous tyrants is a great boost, but yes, a nice gathering like this every now and then will help," he says.

"Why are you three here, in the corner, hiding?" I ask, scanning the other two faces.

"Some of the female Fae keep asking for us to dance with them. We have politely declined but more seemed to find us until we moved here," Wren states.

"Oh, well that was a great idea. I don't know how I would feel about sharing you with another woman. That sounds a little hypocritical, all things considered," I say.

"You are the only woman for us and we don't mind sharing just no more adding men," Flynn remarks with a smile.

To that we all laugh and Kain reappears with two glasses in hand.

"What's so funny?" he asks as he hands me one.

"Just Flynn, no need to worry," I tell him.

Kain takes the open set next to Xavier and asks, "So, are we heading to the human realm?"

All the guys look at me, "I can't leave this place, not yet. How would that look? Leaving right after freeing the realm would also open us up to attack. Besides, no one would trust me if I did that. I was thinking maybe Flynn and Xavier could go to the mortal realm and see if my parents would come here. There is so much in me that wants nothing more than to pack a bag and head to the portal but I have responsibilities here and I'm not just going to skip out on them," I explain.

"If that's what you want, I'm game," Xavier says as Flynn nods.

"That is a great and hard decision, my Love," Wren says, "but it's the right one for now. I will aid them in packing anything they will need for the trek."

"Thank you. Will you guys stay with me until tomorrow afternoon?" I ask. "That way you can rest and I can see you off?"

"As you wish," Xavier and Flynn say at the same time.

Zelle

After a night of dancing and chatting I'm surprised I have enough energy to walk to our suite. Cavill and Jarica take up guard outside the door while Flynn, Kain, Wren, Xavier, and I get ready for bed. I was a little worried about sleeping arrangements, but to my amusement Wren had that covered as well. Seems as though my vampire army built us a double king bed while we were at the party. It's monstrous, taking up more than half the space easily, but I love it.

"I hope you don't think I'm sleeping in the middle," I smirk as I emerge from the layers of purple fabric. "It would take too long to get up to pee!"

"Don't worry, Zelle, we will sleep however you see fit. I'm just happy we will all be in the same bed," Wren laughs as he lays his armor on the small couch near the balcony. The others follow his lead, leaving four piles of gleaming metal on the furniture.

Once we're all down to the bare essentials, my cheeks begin to heat. I've, of course, seen many naked men when I treat injuries, but Kain has been my only lover. Trying not to be awkward, I climb onto the bed and slip under the cover.

"If you'd prefer we can draw straws on who will sleep with you," Kain suggests. "The rest of us could sleep in the connecting sitting room."

"No!" I almost screamed. I can't bear the thought of being separated from any of my men. I lower my voice, "I want you all in here with me, please."

There's a shared look between the men before Kain dims the fairy lights and the three men timidly join me. Xavier is the first at my right side, he's tucked his wings into his body to make things easier. Flynn eases onto the edge of the bed at my left while Kain and Wren kneel at the foot of the bed almost serenely.

"Zelle," Xavier caresses my bottom lip with his thumb, "we'd like it very much if you'd allow us to show you what loving four men can be like. You can of course say no or stop at any time with no ill will."

My heart hammers in my chest as I meet his golden gaze. WIthout his wings creating a shield, I can see the others behind him. Fear and desire both run through my veins like wildfire. Peeking over at Flynn, I melt at the longing written on his face. They've all been so patient. I realize I, too, would like to experience loving my men at once.

"Yes," I whisper, placing a hand over his.

Xavier lets out a long breath before leaning forward and placing his lips against mine. There's an urgency in his kiss that hasn't been there before, it excites me. Tangling my other hand in his hair, I rise up onto my knees.

Heat builds between us. Xavier wraps his arms around me, pressing our bodies as close together as possible in this position. Running a hand along his back, I trace the line where his wings emerge. As if called, they pop out with a snap enfolding us in a white cocoon.

"Zelle," Xavier whispers in a breath between our kisses. His eyes bore into mine, stripping my soul bare before him.

Realizing he's waiting for me to make the first move, I straddle his legs. His hard cock nestles between my nether lips in sweet torture. I want him inside of me. Rocking my hips, I raise the anguish as I slide along his length with my wetness.

"You'll be the death of me," Xavier hisses. Cupping one cheek, he lifts me up to position himself. I gasp in relief as he enters me fully. We find a slow rhythm together, eyes locked. I wrap my arms around his neck for support as my body begins a slow climb toward ecstasy. My muscles tense and I can't help but cry out in pleasure as my body unfolds for Xavier.

His wings snap open just as I reach my zenith. Before I can search with my eyes, I feel a warm body at my back. Arching my neck, I lock lips with Flynn. His hands rove between Xavier and I, caressing my breasts before moving downward.

"Make her cum again so I can follow her," Xavier says with bated breath.

Flynn's only answer is a hum deep in his throat before his mouth devours mine. The sensations of being impaled by one man and fondled by another quickly overwhelm me. Every part of me is on fire. Engulfed in the flames, another climax hits me hard and fast. Pulling my mouth from Flynn's, I cry out. Xavier's thrusts become faster and harder before he stills, grabbing my hips.

"Oh love," he whispers, pulling me to his chest. I nestle for a moment before kissing his cheek and untangling myself. When I turn, Flynn is waiting where I left him. His cheeks are flush and his lips plush from kissing.

"Wren?" I look to my right and catch a glimpse of both Wren and Kain sitting with their backs propped on pillows.

"Yes, my Queen?" he answers with heat in his voice.

"Is it possible to have two of you at once?"

Flynn chuckles, reaching for me and pulling me down onto the bed between Wren and him. "I thought you to be innocent, blondie." He smirks as he covers my body with his. Opening my legs, I arch my back to close the distance between us. Flynn pauses, his cock at my entrance.

"Zelle, are you sure you're ready so soon?" he asks with a serious face.

In answer, I wrap my legs around him and arch my back. With a groan, Flynn grasps my knees and enters me with one aggressive thrust. Watching his chiseled abs roll as he rocks back and forth is sweet agony. He's a vision of sexual prowess above me. Not forgetting Wren, I reach upward until I grasp his neck and pull him toward me. Wren's mouth meets mine and takes greedy possession of my lips.

The snap of Xavier's wings registers in the back of my mind. Hazily, I wonder what Kain and the angel must be doing now. Not wanting to break the kiss to see, I focus on listening. Kain lets out a rumble of pleasure just as Xavier's wings snap again. "I didn't think I'd like this, watching," Kain states. "But it's fucking hot."

"Agreed," Xavier answers with a throaty hum.

Beaming at their responses, I shift my attention back to Wren. His blond hair cascades over my face, tickling my cheek as we kiss. With one hand, I grip his neck, then trace a line down his abs until I find his hardness. When I wrap my palm around the length, he bucks. Touching him makes me feel powerful. The surge of confidence sparks through me, sending waves of pleasure throughout my body.

"Zelle," Flynn pants. "I'm not going to last long with you tightening on me like that."

Parting from the kiss, I lock gazes with my sexy thief. "Then come, I can feel my body waiting to join yours."

His cheeks redden and he falls forward, locking lips with me as his pace quickens. The new angle touches something inside of me that makes me instantly fly apart at the seams. From the tightening of his grip on my shoulder, I'm sure that Flynn is joining my climax. Stars flash before my eyes and my body relaxes. Flynn cups my cheeks and places a final kiss on my lips before. rolling off to the side.

Poor Wren, I hadn't realized I was still gripping his cock. Through heavy lids, I look over to him. He's propped on one arm staring intently, "You're the most beautiful thing in all the realms," he whispers as he takes my hand from its position and kisses my knuckles.

Sad to see him left out, I scoot to his side, throwing a leg over his. Kain pops up, dropping a kiss on my head before sliding off the bed. "I'm going to get snacks!" he says with gusto.

"That is a good idea. Grab some water drops for our Queen as well," Wren says over his shoulder. Then he turns his attention back to me. I've never seen him look so serene. "You should sleep, my Queen. My needs can wait until later."

"But—" I start but he shushes me.

Xavier swoops over and places a warm towel between my legs while handing another to Wren. The two of them clean me from head to toe before tucking me into the sheets. Wren spoons his body around my back and Xavier lays in front of me.

"Rest," Wren says as he wraps an arm around me. "When you wake there will be food and water and as much love making as you choose."

I think about a retort, but it dries on my lips as sleep claims my fully sated body.

※

"I't's been three days," I complain as dusk sets, leaning on the balcony, my eyes on the gates. I will them to open to reveal my men but they stay closed.

When the sigh leaves my lips, Kain and Wren move on either side of me, each wrapping an arm around me.

"They will be back soon," Kain promises.

"I know, my heart just aches from their absences. You two mean the world to me as well. I just like it better when we are all together," I tell them both. I don't favor one of the others, it's as if my heart is incomplete with Flynn and my angel gone.

"You don't owe us an explanation or anything. We know that you love them as you do us. Kain and I get it," Wren says just as a pounding on our chamber doors starts.

"Are we expecting guests?" Kain asks as he removes his arm from me.

I miss his warmth already as I shake my head. "Not that I can recall, but after healing our people these last few nights, everything seems to run together."

Wren pulls me in closer while Kain goes to answer the door.

"I told you that you should take a day or two off in between all the doctoring you've been doing," Wren lectures me again.

"I know, I know," I sigh, "I just can't sit back while people are injured if I can heal them. They were all treated as if they were trash on the bottom of the former Queen's heels, I will not repeat her mistakes."

"There you go over explaining again," Wren laughs.

I just shrug, because I meant every word.

"Umm...Zelle," Kain stammers, "Jarica is at the door. She said that she has what you requested. I'm not sure what it could be as she has it in a bag, but it seems to be bleeding all over the floor."

"Oh good," I exclaim, clapping my hands together as I wiggle from Wren's grip.

"Why are you happy about gore?" Wren asks as they both trail behind me.

"I sent her on a little mission, for the head of my fake mother," I state flatly.

"Oh, that explains it, but why didn't you do it yourself?" Kain asks.

"I knew it would take me time to track her down. I wasn't sure if there was time for that between healing all the Fae. So, I sent Jarica. With her speed, she could do it in half the time as I could and I was correct." I smirk as I face my vampire guard.

"As you requested, the head of Gothel," Jarica says. With no emotion in her words or face, she holds up the bag to me.

I take it from her, just to verify it is Gothel. Peeking inside, I find the blank stare of my former jailor greeting me. To think I believed she was my family.

"Thank you, Jarica," I say, closing the bag and handing it back to her. "Please burn this. I'll get this mess cleaned up."

She nods but doesn't move, "I will tidy up the trail of blood, I made the mess and I intend to clean it."

"If you're sure, I appreciate all you do," I say as she moves back down the hall without another word.

"It's time to dress, the injured Fae will be lining up soon," I say with a yawn.

"Can't I talk you into taking the night off?" Kain asks with a grin.

"Trust me, I would love to, but there are a few Fae I promised to look at their children tonight. I will not let them down," I tell him.

"Fine," Wren says, "but I'm clearing your schedule for tomorrow. You need to replenish your strength."

I concede because I know my consort is right, I feel weary in my bones from using my gift on so many. I've taken on more in an hour than the King ever sent me in a night. A few days off with my guys is just what I need, if only the other two would get their asses back to me.

Wren brings over my gown. I wrinkle my nose when I notice the colors are again purple and pink. Why do the Fae think those are the only colors I wear? The garment is beautiful like all the others, but what I wouldn't give for a green dress, just to shake it up.

I remove my night clothes and step into the garb without a fuss. Kain steps up behind me and laces me in while Wren fetches my brush. In the days since my coronation, my hair has again reached an unmanageable length. I will need to cut it again.

"You two know that I can dress myself right?" I question, accepting my brush.

"What would we do then?" Kain asks, pulling the corset a little too tight.

"I can think of a few things," I comment, winking at him, "I can finish this, you two need to get ready. That is unless you want to go out in front of the kingdom naked?" I say with a sneaky laugh.

Wren and Kain share a look before they both hurry off to change and I have to stifle a laugh. Smiling, I move to the vanity and do what I can to tame my bed head. It's not the worst I've had but I need to remember to braid it before bed from here out.

Hair tamed, I holler back at the guys, "Are you ready?"

"Yes," they reply in unison and both appear in the mirror behind me.

"Then let's not keep our people waiting," I say as I push back from the wooden table.

Kain offers me an arm and I take it. Wren doesn't seem to mind as he leads out of our chambers and to the throne room. Luckily, we have a back way in as there is a line snaking down the hall in our path.

"Seems you were right," Wren states, turning back to wink at me.

"Why does it feel like there is an 'I told you' coming," I joke as we make it to the back doors.

The chamber is empty as I take my seat on the throne, Cavill is kneeling in front of me in a blink of an eye.

"Are you ready to see the Fae, my Queen?" he asks, his red eyes boring into mine.

"Yes, but the next few nights I will rest. Would you please inform the Fae of this? Unless it's life or death, I need to recharge my powers," I inform Cavill.

"Of course," my vampire guard replies.

"You and the others should do the same. All who serve me should take time off," I say sternly. I don't ever want to be like Thayer.

"We don't require rest," Cavill states flatly before he turns to open the throne room doors.

I'm grateful that the vampires can keep the crowds under control or the room would be full of those in need.

"Ready?" Cavill asks again.

"I am, thank you."

※

The night seems to drag on, even with as many of the people I have healed. King Thayer controlled so many, and cared for them naught. Group after group come and I take on their hurts. It leaves me longing for the warmth of my bed and my men.

After hours, I can't contain the yawn.

"Should I tell the rest to come back after your rest?" Cavill asks after helping an older Fae out.

"How many more are there?" I question.

"Do you really want me to go count?" He turns and opens his palms to me.

My face falls, are there really that many out there still? "No, I'm fine. Let's continue." I yawn again.

As he returns to let in the next subject, there is a commotion and the servants around me begin to chatter.

"What's going on?" I ask, standing to try and get a better look into the hall. The only things in view are the tips of two white wings.

"Xavier?" I gasp and take off toward the doors, my heart racing.

The crowd splits before me, revealing my beautiful angel. His wings are spread so that I cannot see behind him, no matter how I crane my neck. "My Queen!" The angel falls to one knee as I approach.

"I'm so happy to see you!" I tumble down into his arms, almost forgetting why I sent him away.

"Love, you might want to stand for the next moment," Xavier kisses my cheek and helps me to my feet.

With his arm around my shoulder, we turn. Flynn dips his head and steps to the side to reveal a stately couple. They wear robes of blue and gold, their brown hair topped with simple crowns.

"Oh, my darling," the woman calls as she opens her arms.

Without thinking, I leave Xavier's side and cross the small steps between my mother and I. Her arms envelop me and a piece of my heart clicks into place. Her hold feels like home. She smells so familiar, it brings tears to my eyes.

"We never gave up hope looking for you," my father whispers as he joins the embrace.

"I can't believe you came," I cry.

"Why wouldn't we? Your father and I have been dreaming of this day since you were taken from us," my mother answers, her voice like a melody.

"Flynn, Xavier come here," I command.

The two approach cautiously, kneeling at my feet.

With joy bursting from my heart, I place a hand on each of their shoulders. "Thank you for this. You've made my biggest wish come true. I can never repay you."

"Your love is more than payment enough," Flynn blushes.

Thank you's and greetings out of the way, I turn to the crowd. "Today is a joyous day! Fae of Wolgast, meet my parents, King and Queen ....?" I stop, confused because I don't know their names or titles.

"King and Queen of Corona," Flynn finishes. "Now, if you would all grant the Queen time to reunite with her family. She will open her arms again to you after much-needed rest."

There's a murmur of joy and congratulations are shouted as the throne room and hall are emptied. Spirits high, I lead my family out to the courtyard. "Jarica, can you have the maids bring some refreshments?" I ask politely.

"Of course." the guard bows before disappearing.

Looking from my right to my left, I can't help but laugh with happiness. I'm surrounded by four men that love me as well as my birth parents. I couldn't ask for a better start to my new life.

The End.

Thank you for reading our adaptation of Rapunzel's story. We hope you loved reading it as much as we loved writing it.

ABOUT THE AUTHOR

ROWAN THALIA

My pen name is Rowan Thalia. I published my first novel on February 14, 2019.

I discovered very early on that I loved writing. Poetry was my first love and form of expression. I've written poems since I was sixteen and have quite the collection by now! Some of them you can find in my two poetry anthologies.

I've always been an avid reader and writer of short stories. My favorite author of all time is Anne Rice. In fact my pen name stems from one of her characters, Rowan, from The Witching Hour.

It wasn't until 2017, that I decided to push through and write a full-length novel. I started Binding Rayne (which went through several title changes at first) but struggled with the direction. In the middle of the first draft, I happened upon the reverse-harem book community on facebook. The complicated romances rooted in my author heart and before long, my book took on a new direction. The Keepers of the Talisman trilogy was born!

Since then, I have written and published many more reverse-harem romance novels, most of them paranormal in genre. Never to be one to sit idle, I've recently opened a second pen name—R. Thalia. With this name, I began the journey of writing my first (non-romance) paranormal thriller. I can't wait to break out and show the book world my full range of capabilities.

Thank you for all of the support and love that has been shown toward my book babies so far, I hope to keep surprising you with bigger and better projects!

Rowan's author page on amazon:
   http://author.to/rowanthalia

And her website:
   www.rowanthalia.com

JENÉE ROBINSON

Jenée Robinson has been married for over 20 years now, has three ornery girls, and lives on a cattle farm.

Writing has always been one of her loves and she's excited to see where it takes her.

She has completed several books, short stories, and has more releasing soon. She is busy writing more, so keep an eye out.

Other than writing, she loves reading and photography.

She's a Harry Potter Nerd and loves the show Supernatural and Captain America.

Jenée's author page on amazon:
https://www.amazon.com/Jenee-Robinson/e/B07BNC33ZB

Made in the USA
Columbia, SC
20 February 2023

12459529R00138